# BROKEN QUEEN

RUINED KINGDOM
BOOK 2

NATASHA KNIGHT

Copyright © 2022 by Natasha Knight

All rights reserved.

No part of this book may be reproduced in any form or by any electronic or mechanical means, including information storage and retrieval systems, without written permission from the author, except for the use of brief quotations in a book review.

This is a work of fiction. Names, characters, places and incidents are either the product of the author's imagination or are used fictitiously, and any resemblance to actual persons, living or dead, business establishments, events, or locales is purely coincidental.

Cover by Deranged Doctor

## ABOUT THIS BOOK

***Betrayal. Destruction. Truth.***

He says you can only rise up once you hit rock bottom. Only be made whole once you're fully broken.

I don't know that there's anything left to break.

Time is running out for me. Enemies are closing in at every turn.

But this time I won't be alone.

One brother has vowed his protection. The other reaffirmed his hatred of me.

Yet they both want me.

But something dark is unraveling inside me.

An event too terrible clawing its way into my consciousness.

And even as things begin to change between us, it's those memories that may undo us all.

> Broken Queen is the second book of the Ruined Kingdom Duet and must be read in order.
>
> You can find Ruined Kingdom in all stores now.

# 1

## VITTORIA

They're everywhere, and they're touching me. Their hands and mouths and tongues are all over me. Their breath is hot at my back. It's sickening. Fingers dig into my hips, keeping them lifted as my knees are forced apart, dragged through shards of broken glass that slice like knives.

I don't scream. I can't. I have no voice. And the music. It's so loud. It pounds against my forehead, which they keep pressed to the floor as the bass vibrates through every cell of my body.

Warmth runs down the inside of my thigh. I've lost control of my bladder.

"Fuck. She's pissing herself."

Someone laughs. I taste vomit. I don't remember throwing up, but I must have. I'm lying in it.

But something shifts in the air then. A door slams. A roar sounds like the battle cry of some wild beast. It's louder than the music and the pounding of blood in my ears.

The fingers digging into my hips loosen just a little. The hand at the back of my head is gone. Attention diverted. A palpable rage rattles the room itself, and an instant later, their hands and their sweaty bodies and disgusting tongues are forced off me.

I should move, but I can't. I'm too scared. Too fucking terrified. I turn my face, laying my cheek in wet, still-warm vomit. Everything hurts. Glass cuts into my knees, my chest. I should get up. Get away while they're distracted. But I'm locked in place on my hands and knees, my face in vomit, my eyes squeezed shut. I don't want to open them. I know I have to, but I can't. I don't want to see, and I can't run.

*What doesn't kill you makes you stronger, princess.*

But no, that's not right. He was wrong. So wrong. I'm not stronger for it. I'm not strong at all.

"How dare you?" a man roars, and I force my eyes to open. A body is flung across the room, knocking over a chair before it slams against the wall. "How dare you touch what's ours?"

Fury. Rage. Raw and unfiltered and wholly violent.

I take in the scene.

Men are scattering, scurrying. Trying like hell to get away. Chairs are knocked over. Boots pound heavy on the concrete floor. One almost makes it to the stairs before he's caught. I lay my body down. Glass digs into my chest, stomach, and thighs, and I wince with the pain, but I can't look away from the chaos. From the two men pummeling the others. Two men taking on an entire room of soldiers.

This is violence like I've never seen before.

No, that's not right. I've seen it once. Blood-splattering, bone-breaking violence. Not a single bullet is fired here, though. Bullets are too easy. Bullets are for when you're outmanned and outmuscled. A single woman against many men. These two, though they may be outmanned, they have enough rage to fill a fucking stadium. And they use their fists. They want to feel the crunching of bone. They want to drench their hands in blood. And all I can do is watch. Just lie there and watch.

Until they finally turn their attention to me.

The dragons who came to my rescue.

One glance. One furious glance. Cold steel eyes and the burning embers of a fire, so opposite, so alike. I try to move, but I can't. I'm cold. My body shivers. The bare concrete floor is freezing.

Footsteps like that of an army charge down the stairs. More men. You can't trust men. I need to get up. I need to run.

I manage to climb to my hands and knees. My body is heavy like I'm dragging my limbs through the thick mud. A few feet from me, Amadeo is smashing his fist again and again into the face of a man on the floor. He's rendered him unrecognizable. I'm transfixed as blood splatters Amadeo's face, hair, and clothes. I wish I were strong like him. I wish I could feel the breaking of bones. Wish I could kill them all with my bare hands.

"Brother," Bastian says, voice hoarse as he wipes the back of his arm across his face, smearing blood. He sets that hand on Amadeo's shoulder. I watch the brothers, so curious about them—these two violent, angry men who are so devoted to one another.

Amadeo is muttering a mantra and beating the man to a pulp. He doesn't hear Bastian. Not yet.

"Amadeo. Stop. Don't fucking kill him. Not yet. That's too good for him," Bastian says.

Someone cuts off the music. The silence that follows is alive with a heart that beats. A man groans, and all around me, I smell the coppery scent of blood over that of basement and puke and piss.

"I plan to take my time," Bastian is saying, and Amadeo stops pounding the unconscious man. His eyes meet mine, and what I see in them, it makes my heart stop. Makes my throat close up so I can't breathe.

He stands, and they both turn their full attention to me. Something gives and a tidal wave of emotion overwhelms me. A keening like that of an animal comes from deep inside my chest, and I think I'm going to choke on it. This thing that won't let me breathe, that's been inside me so long it's a part of me. It's all of it. Everything that's happened. Tonight. The nights before. My father's death. The funeral. That book and what it accuses my brother of. Amadeo and Bastian.

The nightmares of another basement. Another violent night.

A jacket is draped over me, and I smell a familiar aftershave. It's warm. He just took it off. A hand closes on the back of my head, cupping it tenderly. But it's that gentle touch that brings out the animal inside me. It's then I find my voice and scream and scream. I spin as I scream bloody murder grabbing hold of a shard of glass because I will dig it into his eye even if it cuts me through. Even if they kill me for it. But I won't let them touch me. I won't let any of them touch me.

"Fuck!" Glass crunches under Bastian's shoes. He catches my arm and squeezes my wrist, forcing me to drop the glass to the floor. "You're safe. Vittoria. Look at me." I shove against him, and he releases my wrist. The jacket slips from me as I try to scramble away through this carpet of broken bottles.

"Vittoria. Look at me." It's Amadeo's voice now. I'm backed into a corner, the wall cold against my bare skin. "Vittoria."

I claw around me for a weapon. More glass. A gun. Anything. And when he puts his hands on me and gives me a shake, I attack, clawing at his face and arms and screaming like an animal until he slaps me, stunning me.

My head jerks to the side, and I'd fall over if he didn't catch me. Pulling me to him, he presses my face into his chest. My cheek stings from where he hit me, but it has its desired effect. I'm not screaming. Clawing. Attacking like some beast.

"Shh. Quiet now. You're safe." I can't tell if it's Bastian or Amadeo's voice. My arms are behind me, wrists held tight by one brother while the other cradles the back of my head and whispers that I'm safe, I'm all right. I'm safe.

But I'm not all right. I haven't been all right for a very long time. And I've never been safe.

"We need to get her upstairs and out of here," Bastian says. "Away from these men. This place."

Amadeo straightens and lifts me up, cradling me against him. I wrap my arm around his neck and bury my face against him. I taste blood.

*What doesn't kill you makes you stronger, princess.*

I feel my resistance giving way. Hot tears stream down my face as I cry ugly and loud. The smell of the room, of basement and beer and whiskey and violence, is too much, and when that cry is over, I'm so exhausted. Empty. Physically. Emotionally. Mentally. I am so fucking tired, and this emotion has drained the last of my energy. I can't fight anymore. I can't.

Amadeo must feel me yield because he tucks me closer and tells me it'll be all right. He looks down at me, and I meet his eyes for an instant before turning my face back into his chest and burying it there.

"Get them all in the back of the truck," Bastian says. "You know where to take them. No one touches them without my order. Understood?"

"Yes, sir," a soldier answers.

Amadeo begins the climb up the stairs. I open my eyes briefly to see Bastian following, eyes locked on me, so I close mine again, breath heaving as years-old tears stream like never before.

## 2

## AMADEO

"I'll get the kit," Bastian says as I carry Vittoria through the dark house, past the open door of her bedroom and to my own. Adrenaline sends blood pounding through me.

We knew something was wrong the minute we drove through the still-guarded gates of the Naples house. Bastian commented on how dark the house was as the thought formed in my own mind. I'd been thinking about Sonny's strange mention of one of our houses being attacked. About rats. Was it his warning? Had he already ordered the attack while we were at the Ravello house talking? While he was visiting and making nice with mom? When we walked through the front doors, we saw right away that less soldiers were inside than should have been. The house was dark. Too dark. And the stink of cigarettes, aggression, and fear permeated from the basement.

But those soldiers down there, they were ours.

We were attacked from within, and Vittoria was their target. I failed to protect her as I promised I would.

Bastian draws the blankets back, and I lay her on the bed. The jacket falls open, and I see the sudden panic in her eyes as she looks up at me. But her eyes are unfocused, so it's not me she sees. She tries to claw at me again, making that strange keening sound like a wounded animal cornered but still fighting.

"It's me, Vittoria. It's Amadeo," I tell her, seeing the print of my own hand on her pale cheek, feeling the guilt of having injured her. I did it to draw her out of her head, but still, I hurt her.

"Those men would have done worse," Bastian says when he sees what I'm looking at. He sets the black duffel on the foot of the bed. He's washed his hands and discarded his bloodied T-shirt for a clean one, but he missed a smear of blood on his jaw. Unzipping the duffel, he takes one of the syringes out. There are half a dozen because we'd prepared for taking her. The instant Vittoria sees it, her strength renews and she redoubles her fight.

"No one is going to hurt you, but we need to get the glass out," I tell her, folding her arms across her chest and pressing them down. Wide, wild eyes stare up at me. She's shaking her head, and I'm not sure she hears me as she struggles, her eyes darting from me to Bastian to the syringe.

"Her neck," Bastian says calmly once he's pushed the air from the barrel.

"No! No!"

I keep a tight hold of her and turn her face away while Bastian finds the injection site and pushes the needle in.

Vittoria whines, but I keep her steady until he's done.

Her gaze moves to Bastian, then to me, and I can see her struggling to keep her eyes open as her arms fall to her sides when I release them.

I cup her face with both hands, brushing her hair back. "Vittoria. I promise you no one will hurt you again. I swear it." I say it with a ferocity that burns in my gut as she struggles to focus. "Close your eyes and sleep. We need to get you cleaned up. It's better this way. Trust me."

She makes a sound, still fighting the drug, but it won't take long to do its work, and within moments, she's still.

"Jesus." Bastian sets the syringe aside and pushes his hand through his hair. He exhales, tension evident on his face. "I'm going to fucking kill those men."

He paces the room, processing, expression grave every time it lands on the now-unconscious Vittoria.

I turn back to her. She's bruised and cut, and it's my fault. I left her unprotected. I thought I was in control, but I was not, and she paid the price for my failure.

Were we in time? Or did they hurt her more deeply and take the thing that would break her?

"I told her she had my protection," I say.

Bastian presses a hand to my shoulder. "*Our* protection, brother."

I think of Hannah. Hannah at the mercy of Lucien Russo.

A girl at the mercy of a man.

I brush hair from Vittoria's forehead, my fingers coming away bloody.

A woman at the mercy of a dozen men.

"Go wash the blood off your hands, Amadeo," Bastian tells me.

I don't move. I don't want to leave her.

"I'll be with her. Go."

I go into the bathroom and close the door behind me. After stripping off and trashing my ruined shirt, I wash my hands, which are sticky with blood up to my elbows. A glance at my reflection tells me I'd better wash my face, too, and I do, then look at myself.

This was Sonny. I have no doubt. But our soldiers betrayed us. Men who are supposedly loyal to my brother and me. How many more traitors lie within?

I dry my hands and face. There's more blood to wash off, but I'll do it after I'm done cleaning her. I return to the bedroom to find Bastian looking her over, already having started.

She's cut up badly at her hands and knees, her feet. Her forehead where they must have pushed her face down. Shards are stuck to her stomach, thighs and chest, too, but those don't look as bad.

"They're mostly shallow. It looks worse than it is,"

Bastian says as we get to work picking the glass out with tweezers and depositing the shards into a bowl.

"That's not the damage I'm worried about," I say.

"We were in time," he says without looking at me.

"You don't know that." Silence settles between us. "She was under my protection."

"*Our* protection. And in case you've forgotten, we're at war, brother. Have been since the day grandfather died. Hell, since Geno Russo walked into our kitchen when we were just kids. This is a reminder. She'll be fine. She's strong like a fucking dandelion. They will sprout up after the earth is razed to rubble."

It's quiet for a long time, and I can't help looking at Vittoria's face as she sleeps. I hope it's a dreamless sleep. I remember the nightmare she'd had the night I'd watched her. She'd fought so hard that I could see it in the muted movements of her body.

"Let's roll her over."

We roll her gently onto her stomach but don't find much glass here. A few cuts but the worst are the bruises in the shape of fingers digging into her hips.

"I'm going to fucking kill them with my bare hands," Bastian says.

"You're going to have to get in line."

Once she's on her back again, Bastian pulls her legs apart. I am relieved not to see any bruising, blood, or anything that might suggest they'd gotten as far as that. But we won't know for sure until she wakes up.

"It looks like we were in time to stop that at least," Bastian says.

I breathe a sigh. It's been a long fucking day. Bastian and I clean her with wet, soapy cloths, and I slip one of my shirts on her.

"I'll take her to your room," I tell him when I see the state of the bed.

Bastian nods, and I lift Vittoria. She's light and so fragile. The thought of those men with their hands on her fills me with a rage I'm not sure I'll be able to control when I see them.

Once in Bastian's room, he pulls the blankets on his bed back, and I lay her down. She doesn't move as I cover her and turn to the door just as Jarno appears.

Bastian and I step out into the hallway and pull the door closed.

"Six of our men are dead," Jarno says. "Bullet to the back of the head."

I grit my jaw.

"The ones from the basement?" Bastian asks when I can't because all I can see is the unconscious woman just beyond that door with my handprint burning red on her cheek.

"On their way to the ruined barn," Jarno answers.

"We need more soldiers on-site here and at the Ravello house," Bastian says.

"Already working on it with Bruno."

"Good. Let us know when it's done," Bastian says.

"Where is my uncle?" I ask with a snarl.

"Positano. At the woman's house," Jarno says.

"Make sure he stays there. I don't fucking care what it takes."

## 3

## BASTIAN

It's been a very long time since I've slept beside someone. Since I was a kid. The nightmares began soon after Hannah's funeral. The visit by the Russos. Mom kept me with her when they came, which was so often it forced my father out of their bed. I wonder if that wasn't another moment in the deterioration of our lives that I'm responsible for. But it would help. Mom would whisper to me that I was all right. That those men weren't coming back.

By the time I was twelve, though, that stopped. I was too old to go running to Mommy with every nightmare. Sometimes I'd go to Amadeo's room and sleep on the floor there. He made a game of it, acting like it was just a normal sleepover. He'd leave my sleeping bag in the corner so I never felt embarrassed or ashamed. Never felt like I was a pussy for having the nightmares or not being stronger like him.

Vittoria doesn't sleep peacefully. At first, I think it's

the events of the evening causing the nightmares, but as I listen, I'm not sure. The drug mutes things, though, that I know. Her slurred words mean I only pick up bits and pieces, recognizing *Lucien* and *Daddy*. Both of those only serve to anger me, but then I look at all the cuts and bruises and I soften, trying to wake her, at least nudge her out of the nightmare.

By morning, she's quiet. It's when I get a few hours of sleep myself and wake up just as Vittoria begins to stir. She rubs her eyes, rolling onto her side, her back to me. I know the moment she opens them and realizes she doesn't know where she is because she stiffens.

"Morning, Dandelion."

She sits up with a gasp, wincing at the pain. I'm guessing headache in addition to the bruises. Panic and confusion make her sapphire eyes go wide and wild, and I put up both hands, palms to her.

"You're safe. I'm not going to hurt you."

She glances at my bare shoulders and arms, then looks down at herself and sees she's dressed. She takes in all the bandages, and I wonder what she remembers. Surely, she remembers. After a very long minute, she draws her knees to her chest and the blankets along with them, shuddering even though it's warm.

"Where are they?" she asks without looking at me.

I lie with my elbow on my pillow, head in my hand watching her. "Away from here."

That makes her look at me. Her eyes wander to my chest, down to the tattoo over my heart. She's seen it before but didn't have a chance to study it. It's a set of heavily imbalanced scales. A heart on one dish, a skull in the other, and dandelions scattered throughout. The text underneath reads: I will carry out great vengeance on them and punish them in my wrath.

"Ezekiel. I don't know the verse," I say.

"25:17"

"*Pulp Fiction*?"

"The Bible."

With a grin, I climb out of bed. Her eyes follow me as I move to the bathroom. I don't close the door but switch on the shower. I strip off my briefs and brush my teeth, then step under the flow. I give her time to leave my room and go to my brother. I left the door unlocked. But when I'm done, I'm surprised to find her sitting exactly where I left her.

Drying off, I walk into the closet to pull on a pair of jeans and a T-shirt.

"Where is Amadeo?" she asks when I'm back in the bedroom.

"He's around. How do you feel?"

"Like I was run over by a truck."

"Sounds about right." I walk into the bathroom and return with two pills and a glass of water. "Here."

"What are they?"

"Aspirin. Unless you want something stronger."

She takes the pills and swallows them with some water, then drains the whole glass. "What did you give me last night?"

"Just a sedative to relax you."

"It knocked me out."

"We needed to pick the glass out, and you were pretty out of it."

She drops her gaze, then pushes a hand into her hair.

"Hey. You're all right, Dandelion."

She snorts, then looks up at me. "Why did you help me?"

"What kind of question is that?"

She shrugs a shoulder.

"You mean why didn't we let them rape you?" The word triggers a visceral response from her. "What do you think we are? Dogs?"

"He said you ordered it. You and your brother. Was I supposed to learn a lesson?"

My hands fist at my sides. "Who said that?"

"I don't know his name. The one who brought me down."

"Well, he fucking lied." I hear the anger in my voice. The silence that follows is broken by Amadeo when he walks in. We both turn to look at him. He's freshly showered but looks like shit. Like he didn't sleep all night.

"Morning." His forehead is furrowed as he takes her in. "How do you feel?"

She doesn't bother to answer him but glares instead. "If last night is any indication of how your protection works, I want out. I want Emma out. Now."

His jaw tightens. "It won't happen again."

"And I should just believe you?"

"They'll be punished. This morning."

"I want out!"

"That can't happen, and you know it."

She shakes her head, the whites of her eyes growing pink as they fill with tears she is quick to wipe away.

"Do we need to call a doctor in, Vittoria?" I ask, changing the subject.

"What?"

I glance at Amadeo, then turn back to her. "Did they... hurt you? Touch you?"

She stares up at me, all wide eyes and innocence. And fuck. I don't want to feel anything for her but hate. I try to tell myself it's pity, but I know better. Something inside me wants to protect her. A thing that feels she's mine to protect.

I stand by what I said to Amadeo last night. She is strong—a survivor—and something dark made her that. I know it in my gut. And I'm guessing that missing year Amadeo mentioned is it.

When she's quiet longer than I like, I feel my muscles tighten. Feel a rage build inside me.

"Did they touch you?" I say through my teeth.

She shakes her head and hugs her knees, pressing her eyes into them I assume to stop the inevitable tears.

"Are you sure?" Amadeo asks, clearly confused by how she answered. "You understand it's not your fault—"

"I'm not fucking stupid," she snaps furiously. "I know it's not my fault. But they didn't rape me. They didn't get the chance, so I guess I have you both to thank for that. Oh wait, you put me in a situation where they could get to me in the first place, so maybe not."

I know she's scared. What happened has terrified her more than she'll ever admit to us or maybe even to herself. And she's right—we don't deserve her gratitude.

She looks back and forth between us. "Where are they?"

"You don't have to worry about them. We'll take care of them."

"They're your soldiers."

"That's complicated."

"Complicated how?"

"Our uncle has men who are still loyal to him," I tell her.

She studies me, then Amadeo but doesn't ask any questions.

"They won't hurt you again. You don't have to worry about them," Amadeo says.

"How can you be sure?" she asks us.

"I'm sure because they will be executed this morning," I answer her.

For a moment, she seems surprised by this. Or perhaps it's the violence of what is to come. I don't know. This is our world. I need to remember it's not hers. Even if it was her father's and her brother's, she has been shielded from it.

She searches my eyes, a line forming between her eyebrows.

"For fuck's sake, please tell me it's not pity you feel for them," I say.

"Oh no, it's not pity," she says, looking determined. Any vulnerability is gone, and a strange, almost unhinged sheen comes over her eyes. "I want to be there."

Amadeo and I glance at each other. He has an eyebrow raised, and I'm sure my expression matches his.

"I mean it," she says, her voice cold. "I want to be there. I have a right."

"No, Dandelion."

"I want to see. I'm owed that, don't you think? After what they did to me?"

"She has a point," I say.

Amadeo shakes his head. "Violence like what they'll suffer you won't be able to forget—"

"I won't forget the violence I already suffered. At least I can know they got what they deserved."

"Vittoria," Amadeo starts but stops when she slides her legs over the side of the bed and stands, wincing when she puts weight on her feet. He takes a step toward her, but she shakes her head and pushes through the pain. I have a feeling this girl would walk over hot coals to get what she wants. I'm right. She may be broken but whatever happened to her made her strong. It made her a survivor.

"I need to see it done," she says to me, perhaps

sensing an ally. She comes to stand at my side and turns to Amadeo. "I need it."

"Our little Dandelion has a dark side, brother." I shift my gaze to hers and inside her eyes I see the remnants of the nightmares. The shredded, broken look of them. The girl is damaged—more than we could have known—and that damage calls to me. The ugliness on the inside, so opposite the beauty on the outside. I want to uncover the layers and see that darkness. Touch the tatters of her.

I wrap a hand around the back of her neck. She startles but settles into my grip, holding my gaze for a long moment. Something passes between us, and our mutual hate is set aside, at least for the moment. We both turn to Amadeo.

"I'm with her," I tell him. "She goes."

He studies us both. If he refuses to take her, I'll take her myself. But he won't refuse. He sees what I'm seeing too. And the wounded creature inside her is as irresistible to him as it is to me.

## 4

## VITTORIA

I ride in the front with the brothers this time. Strapped into the middle of the seat, I feel them on either side of me. Something has shifted between us. Hell, maybe it's my crazy brain. Another connection zapped.

I remember the strange image that split my mind when they held me down. A memory like the dandelions but this one is too vivid. Too terribly visceral. The one of the kitchen in the house where I picked the dandelions isn't hidden as deeply as this one. This one is like a locked box of the strongest steel. I can't nudge the lid open, can't even peek inside, but after what I glimpsed last night, I'm not sure I want to.

We get to a ruin of what must have once been a large house in the outskirts of town. Soldiers stand guard near the broken-down gate that we drive through. I follow the brothers out of the SUV, wincing with each step. The bottoms of my feet are badly cut, but I swallow the pain whole.

*"What doesn't kill you makes you stronger, princess."*

It's my father's voice in my head. Like he's standing right here.

That strange sequence of images comes again and stops me in my tracks. Men in a room. Me in that room. Someone laughing. A laugh I know. One I hate. And then my father's voice as he lifts me in his arms.

*"What doesn't kill you makes you stronger, princess."*

"Vittoria."

The sun beats down hot like a desert. I look up at it, blinded by it. A bead of sweat runs down the back of my neck.

"Vittoria?"

I blink as the world spins and follow the voice to see both Amadeo and Bastian stopped several paces ahead of me. I'm leaning on a tree trunk, bent double.

"What is it?" Bastian asks.

"Nothing," I say as he approaches because I don't know what the fuck that was. "I just... tripped."

He tilts my chin up, clearly not buying my excuse. "What is it?"

"Nothing."

"Getting cold feet?"

I steel myself. "No." I tug out of his grasp and bypass him to walk toward the large barn past the ruin, where I see soldiers standing guard. Amadeo and Bastian join me within moments with their longer stride. A guard opens the barn door, and the men inside squint into the bright light. We enter, and the first thing I note is the smell of rot. I don't know how long ago this place was in use, but something stinks. The scent is barely masked by that of blood and animals.

"Line them up," Amadeo orders.

Soldiers move into action, and a few moments later, eleven men kneel before us in various states of distress, all with their arms bound behind their backs.

"Where's the twelfth?"

A soldier gestures to the corner where a body lies unmoving, flies already buzzing as they feed.

My stomach turns, but I swallow that down too. I'll swallow it all because what doesn't kill me has to make me stronger, or I'm finished. And it's not just about me anymore. There's my little sister to consider.

But I shudder all the same at the memory the words conjure.

Amadeo and Bastian walk along the line of kneeling men looking at each one, remarking on some. When one of them, the one who'd pulled the beer out of the cooler, spits at Bastian's feet, Bastian backhands him so hard that the man topples backward, and a soldier has to haul him upright. The next time he spits, it's more a drooling of a bloody tooth.

Amadeo starts at one end of the line. Taking his pistol out of its shoulder holster, he presses it so hard against the first man's forehead that his neck is forced back at a painful angle. "Who ordered the attack?" he asks.

"Nobody."

Without hesitating, Amadeo pulls the trigger. I jump as the man drops, and Amadeo moves to the next one like this is the most natural thing on earth to him. Bastian's eyes burn into me, but I can't drag my gaze from Amadeo's broad back. His merciless justice.

He asks the next man the same question. The man looks terrified, and his eyes meet mine momentarily. "I'm sorry. I didn't know. He said—"

A gunshot cuts him off, and my heart beats double-time.

It's the third one's turn. Same question. This one looks at his two dead buddies, then up at the brothers and me. Then into the barrel of Amadeo's gun.

"Who ordered the attack?" Amadeo repeats. I hear the impatience in his voice.

"I don't know. He said... he said..." The butt of Amadeo's gun across his temple stops his stuttering. He shakes his head, clearly dazed. "I don't know. He said you did."

Amadeo's gun goes off again. Three down. Eight to go. Should I be feeling sick at this display of power and violence? This death? I don't. I feel calm. Peaceful almost. What does that say about me?

Amadeo turns to me. "Do any of them stand out?"

I swallow as I scan their faces. Remembering the one who pulled me onto his lap and began tearing my dress, I point at him. Bastian goes to him, aims his weapon, and shoots him in the shoulder. The man screams as he falls backward. He's righted almost immediately by one of their soldiers, and Bastian shoots the other shoulder before targeting his knees. He leaves the man moaning in agony on the ground.

"Anyone else?" he casually asks me.

Oh yeah. There's one other. I walk up to that one. The one who called me princess. Who dragged me into that room and threw me down the stairs.

The brother's watch, Bastian coming to my side as the kneeling man glares up at me. I look him deep in the eyes because I want to remember him. Remember men like him. They all have one thing in common. Every last one of them. Their eyes are flat. Dead. Like Sonny Caballero's eyes.

*Like my brother's eyes.*

I block the thought as soon as it manifests, and without a moment's hesitation, I snatch the gun from Bastian's hand and shoot. I aim for the kneeling man's stomach, and I shoot and shoot and shoot until no bullets remain. I shoot until the weapon simply *clicks, clicks, clicks*.

The man lies at my feet, his body riddled with bullets, his blood staining my face, my clothes, my hands. It's in my mouth, and I swallow it, taste his death. I stand watching until I'm lifted off my feet and dragged away from that barn, out of the room of the massacre that follows my departure.

And as I'm loaded into an SUV, my wrists bound, I think how Amadeo was right. I will never forget this day. This violence I've done.

## 5

## AMADEO

"Have you lost your fucking mind?" I climb into the driver's side of the SUV. Bastian unlocks the cuff tethering her to the handle above the window. He locks it around her other wrist and takes the passenger seat. His phone is ringing, but he doesn't answer it.

"Get these off me," she says, tugging to get free of him.

Bastian easily keeps her bound wrists in one of his hands.

"Answer me," I tell her, stopping just out of the gate to look at her. "Have you lost your goddamned mind?"

She turns her narrowed eyes to me. "I didn't do anything worse than he'd have done to me. In fact, I showed mercy by killing him quickly."

"Christ," I mutter while Bastian remains silent. I try to read her and figure out where her head is. She's under severe stress. Traumatized. But fuck, taking the gun and shooting holes into that man is not how I expect her to react. "You don't understand, Dandelion."

"I understand just fine. That man delivered me to those others to be raped."

"It shouldn't have been you," I add.

She snatches her hands from Bastian's grip, closes them over the steering wheel, and tugs.

"Are you fucking insane?" I yell over the screaming of brakes and honking of horns as I right the SUV in our lane and Bastian regains control of her. She struggles against him the whole way home, and once we get there, he lifts her out and carries her up the stairs to her bedroom. He sets her on her feet, and she stumbles backward to get away from us.

"Get these off me!"

Bastian's phone rings again, and he walks out of the room to take the call.

I stalk toward her, taking her arm and walking her into the bathroom where I switch on the shower and force her under the flow fully clothed.

"What are you doing? Stop!" she yells, sputtering as water pours over her head and face. I tear at the clothes she's wearing, stripping her naked.

"I'm cleaning the fucking blood off you. Look at yourself."

"He deserved it! He deserved worse!"

"Oh, I know he did. And he would have gotten it. But it shouldn't have been you. Don't you understand that?" I shake her, pressing her into the wall. I keep her there with one hand while I strip off my shirt with the other. Her nipples pebble and press against my chest when I step closer, and the fingernails of her locked hands scratch my chest and face.

"I'd do it again in a heartbeat! And I'll do it to you, too!"

"For fuck's sake, you're fucking mad!" I draw her bound arms over her head. We're so fucking close, her naked body against mine, skin to skin, that I'm breathing in the air she exhales. But behind the raw fury in her eyes, I see the bruised pieces of the girl she is beneath. The vulnerable, broken thing. It's not what I'm expecting. "It shouldn't have been you, little Dandelion."

"I had every right!"

I shake my head. Yes, she had very right. But it shouldn't have been her.

She's confused, angry, raging, blinking through water spilling over her face as that man's blood washes away, and I can see the damage in her. I can fucking see it clear as fucking day. It's written on her face and in that electric blue of her eyes. I smash my mouth over hers, heat and rage burning like an inferno. Her teeth snap at my lips, and I take it. I want it, want her fury. Because it is the essence of her.

Water drills against our skin, and when I draw back this time, I see how dark her eyes have gone. See how she's looking at me. I want her. Fuck, I want her. I need her. Need so much more of her. This furious woman. This vengeful, violent, broken thing.

I kiss her deeply, welcoming the sinking of her

teeth into my lips, tasting her along with the copper of blood. Is it hers, the man she killed? Or mine? She moans against my mouth, sucking on the lip she tore with her teeth. I'm angry, fucking furious at her. At myself. Raging for not having seen what was happening or where her head was. She shouldn't have been there at all. Shouldn't have been the one to do it. To pull the trigger. Once your hands have blood on them, no amount of scrubbing can wash it off. That taint will follow her forever. Cling to her. Damn her.

I press her wrists to the wall, and it takes all I have to break our kiss. Breath ragged, I rest my forehead against hers as I get myself under control. After long minutes, I draw back far enough to look at her, and our eyes lock. I loosen my grip on her hands, and she drops her arms to my shoulders with her bound wrists behind my head.

She's panting, and I'm hard against her. I want this. Need it. And I think she does too. But I draw farther back. I can't. Not now. Not when she's not in her right mind.

"You shouldn't have done it," I say quietly. I'm not sure she hears my words over the shower stream and our breathing. "It shouldn't have been you. Because taking a life, Dandelion, marks your soul. It locks yours with that of the one you stole."

At that, her rage dissipates into something else. Something old. Water catches on her lashes as we stare at one another and I think this may be the most honest moment we've shared. And the most vulnerable.

"I don't care," she says meekly as a tear slips from her eye.

"Well, I do."

Her eyes search mine, and in hers, I see confusion. She leans her face toward mine and kisses my mouth. It's a tender, testing kiss, but I pull away.

"What happened to you out there? Before the barn." She turns away, but I force her to look back at me. "Tell me."

She gives an almost imperceptible shake of her head, and at that moment, she looks so young and so fucking vulnerable it's almost startling.

"I should have been the one to kill him. It was my responsibility to protect you. And I should have pulled the trigger." What's one more soul? Because that's why I'm angry. That and this strange connection we now have. Me and this girl. The blood of my enemy. And what I should do is hate her. I should use her body, take my fill of her, and hate her.

But it's not hate I feel. Not even fucking close.

We're connected. We are the same in some cruel way fate has of fucking with us and driving us to the brink. And that knowledge is what has me lifting her arms from around my neck. Has me stepping back and, with all the strength I have in me, walking away.

## 6

## BASTIAN

My brother's shoulder bumps mine when I walk into the bedroom as he stalks out, shirtless, the clothes he's still wearing soaked through. His forehead is creased, eyes cast straight ahead. Unseeing. Or unwilling to see.

He disappears down the hall and I hear the shower switch off. I walk into Vittoria's bedroom to the bathroom where a naked, still handcuffed Vittoria stumbles, disoriented from the shower. She leaves a pool of water as she crosses the room to pick up a folded towel from the stack. As she stands facing away from me, I'm not sure she realizes I'm there. Staring straight ahead, she's unmoving as water drips down her back.

I wait until she turns toward me. She doesn't startle, so maybe she did know I was here. Her eyes lock on mine, but I can't read her. No, it's not that I can't read her. It's that what I see is her own confusion. I watch her, not seeing this naked girl before me but the one in that barn. The one who snatched my gun from me and fired half a dozen bullet holes into that man. He deserved to die. Absolutely. But for her to have done it? And for me to have watched her face as she did it? Her eyes? It was a strange, dark thing. A thing I'm not sure I understand.

My brother's words echo.

*"She belongs to us now. And we look after what is ours."*

"What happened?" I ask her.

She doesn't look looked after. If he'd touched her, she would have carved out his eyes. She's a fighter. A survivor. And I know Amadeo. He wouldn't have touched her, not given what just happened. But there's something about her that neither my brother nor I expected. She's under his skin—mine too—and pushing our buttons when I don't even think she means to.

Vittoria blinks, then shakes her head to clear whatever thought lingers there. My brother, I guess.

"He deserved to die," she mutters.

I shake my head. "Not that. I mean in there. With Amadeo. What happened?"

She doesn't answer. I move toward her, taking the towel and wrapping it around her shoulders. Her wrists are still bound by the handcuffs. I dry her, squeezing the water from her hair first, then drying her shoulders, her back and arms, her chest, stomach, legs. The blood is gone. Washed away. If only it were that simple.

She stands still as I clean her, eyes never moving from my own. She doesn't answer me. And all I can think is that this girl, this woman, is damaged.

"I'm tired. I want to sleep," she says.

"What happened with my brother?"

"Nothing."

I grit my teeth. "Dandelion."

"Maybe you should ask him." She takes a step away from me, but I catch her arm and draw her back.

"I'm asking you."

Her expression changes, that blankness giving way to something else, something that makes her appear younger than she is. Her forehead creases. There's that confusion again.

"He kissed me."

I guess I'm not expecting that. A kiss. I don't know why this bothers me, but as I watch the line form between her eyebrows, I know she's bothered too. I wonder if maybe we're under her skin too.

With the towel at her back, I lift her. She doesn't resist as I carry her to the bed and lay her down. From my pocket, I take out the key to the cuffs and unlock them. Slipping them off, I secure one around a rung of the headboard. We may need it later.

She looks at it, then at me.

I take the towel out from under her. My gaze sweeps over her small breasts, the taut nipples, and her slender body with its long, lean legs and arms. All that milky skin is still beautiful, even with all the bandages, the cuts, and the bruises. I want to touch her. Touch every inch of her. But I would only dirty her.

On the finger of her left hand is the sparkling diamond ring. I take that hand and wipe away a smear of red on the polished, perfect stone.

She is my brother's wife. It's only on paper, though. I know that, don't I? It's necessary for what needs to happen next. She belongs to us both. When my uncle asked if it bothered me, though, that it's Amadeo and not me? The truth of it is yes. Yes, it does. Did. I don't fucking know.

I shake my head to clear it, to banish the thoughts. This strange feeling in my gut that accompanies them.

Jealousy.

No, not jealousy. I need to remember he's doing it for our cause. It's necessary. And I need to keep that cause in the forefront of my mind and make sure he does too.

I will talk to Amadeo. Make sure he doesn't lose sight of who she is, even given what just happened. We can't forget what her family did. I will ensure my brother and I both remember the endgame because I'm afraid she has the power to make us forget.

Her body shudders. I set her hand on her stomach and look at mine on top of it. Mine is big and calloused, tanned by the constant sunshine. Beauty and her beasts. I draw the blanket over her as the events of the morning replay in my mind's eye. The stench of the barn. The kneeling men. Her face. Her eyes. The moments before, outside, when I turned to find her leaning against the tree, doubled over and panting. Not there at all for a blink. She had the same look in her eyes at that moment as when she snatched my pistol and gunned down her attacker. Her would-be rapist.

"What happened to you?" I ask her, watching her eyes all along. "What made you like this?"

She watches me, too, then turns her head away. "I'm tired."

"No. Look at me." When she doesn't, I take her chin and make her look. "Something happened to you. What was it?"

Her eyes search mine as I explore hers for answers. The brilliant jewel blue grows cloudy, the whites growing pink as they water. Tears slide out of the corner of each eye and slip over her temples. She doesn't try to cover them. She doesn't have the energy to. She's using up her reserves to hide herself from me.

"Tell me what happened to you." My voice is quieter, but I want to know. I want more than anything to know what it was that broke her.

Her expression changes, hardening, her jaw setting. "What doesn't kill you makes you stronger," she says flatly, not like herself at all, and tugs free. I let her roll over onto her side, her back to me. "I'm tired."

"Killing a man will do that to you." I draw the blanket up over her narrow shoulders and lean close to her ear, combing her hair back with my fingers. "I'm going to find out, Dandelion."

No response. Utter stillness in fact. She's holding

her breath. What will happen when I leave this room? Will she break down and sob? Maybe. But I know one thing. It won't be remorse for what she did to that man. Our dandelion is dark. And I will uncover what made her that. *Who* made her that.

# 7

## AMADEO

"You all right?" Bastian asks as we pull out of the gates and head toward Positano, where Sonny visits one of his regular whores. She's apparently become such a favorite that he bought the house for her. She must be a hell of a fuck. Although she is all of eighteen while he's in his late fifties.

When I glance at Bastian, I catch my reflection in the rearview mirror and notice how the line between my eyebrows has deepened. I merge into traffic, two more SUVs following ours. Jarno has men stationed nearer the woman's house as well.

"I'll be fine. It's fucked up, that's all."

"No shit."

"Bruno arranged a meeting with Tilbury while we're in New York by the way."

"How did he do that?"

"Told the doctor our sister was in need of his services." I know at the mention of sister, Bastian thinks of Hannah. I wonder what he remembers of her. It's strange how memories fade. How the faces of the dead fade.

"You think it'll explain what happened in the barn?"

I shrug a shoulder. "Maybe. Give us a clue at least."

"I don't think even she has a clue."

"It's the missing year. I know it in my gut."

We arrive at the woman's house an hour and a half later. It's a small cottage outside of town that Sonny gifted her. It's nice with access to the water. No gates here. When our entourage parks along the edges of the steep, narrow road leading to the entrance, Sonny's two soldiers who stand casually at the front doors straighten, alerted. One disappears inside. He'll announce our arrival. I'm surprised there aren't more. Sonny usually travels with an entourage like he's the fucking king.

Bastian and I climb out of the SUV with our soldiers, who fan out around the property. I don't expect Sonny to make a run for it, but it's time to put him in his place.

Bastian and I head toward the front entrance. The man standing as the lone sentry looks at us, then at the men behind us. He hesitates, unsure whether or not to block our entrance or draw his weapon.

"Don't," I tell him. He's outnumbered, and he's not completely stupid.

"What the hell is the meaning of this?" Sonny demands, coming through the door as he tugs his shirt over his head. I catch a glimpse of his hairy, round stomach I wish I didn't. He stops short when he sees the number of men assembled.

"Uncle," I say by way of greeting. Bastian and I climb the stairs. Sonny stands his ground, and I walk right up to him. The man at his back puts a hand on the butt of his pistol. "Tell your man to stand down."

Sonny's gaze moves over my shoulder again. I guess he's counting my men. He turns to his soldier and nods, and the man folds his hands in front of him.

"Aren't you going to invite us in?" Bastian asks.

Sonny steps aside, and we enter. I take in the living room. It's overcrowded, every surface covered with something gilded and hideous. A woman rushes out of the bedroom wearing what I'm sure is the smallest bikini ever made. She's pulling on a wrap and her long hair is loose down her back, her lipstick smeared. She stops dead when she sees us all.

"Nadia, right?" Bastian says, looking her over. She tugs her wrap closer and shifts her gaze to Sonny. "Did we interrupt?" he asks her. "You've got a little something," he starts, pointing at her mouth.

The woman flushes and wipes the corner of her mouth.

"What the fuck is the meaning of this, Amadeo?" Sonny asks.

"We're going to need you to leave," Bastian tells the woman and makes a point of taking out his wallet and unfolding a couple hundred-dollar bills. He holds them out to her, and her gaze shifts from Bastian to the money then to Sonny.

"This is my house," she says stupidly.

"Yeah, well, if you'd rather stay," Bastian tells her. Tucking his hand into his pocket, he pushes his jacket back so she can see his pistol.

"Nadia. Go," Sonny says.

"Yes, Nadia. Go." Bastian takes more bills from his wallet. I don't miss the way my uncle looks at her. It's certainly not like him to care about anyone other than himself. "We'll try not to make a mess," Bastian tells her with a grin that quickly disappears as he gestures for her to exit. She gives Sonny one more look before taking the money and heading to the door, her heels clicking all the way. "Your wife know about her? Or the dozen others? I do hope you're using a condom, Uncle."

"Explain yourselves," Sonny says once she's gone. "You can't just charge in here like you own the fucking place—"

"My wife was attacked."

Sonny's face gives nothing away. He doesn't even blink.

"She's fine, thanks for asking," Bastian says, moving to close the windows and blinds. Sonny doesn't miss what he's doing.

"An attack on your wife has nothing to do with me," he says.

"No?"

"Of course not. What reason would I have to attack her?"

"To show us you can," I say. "Six of our men were executed."

His eyes narrow.

"Twelve of yours are dead."

"It wasn't me, nephew," he says, sitting on the couch casually, too casually.

I sit on the edge of the coffee table.

His eyes narrow, but he also leans away. He's nervous.

"If it wasn't you, then who was it?"

He shrugs a shoulder. "You have many enemies. Where should I begin?"

"Uncle, have you ever considered just telling the truth?" Bastian asks, coming up behind him and setting the muzzle of his gun to the back of Sonny's head. Sonny doesn't blink. I hold eye contact with him. When Bastian cocks the gun, Sonny flinches. "Say the word, brother."

"Why don't you have more soldiers with you?" I ask him, truly curious. "You don't normally travel without an entourage."

"Nadia doesn't like it."

"Ah. And you like Nadia."

He simply stares at me, eyes blank.

"You do realize she's only here for the money, right?"

"She's not like that."

Bastian snorts. "Of course, she's not."

"It wasn't me," Sonny says, ignoring Bastian. "I didn't order an attack on your wife."

I smile. "No?"

"No."

"All right then." I stand. "Everyone out."

Bastian steps backward, putting his gun away. Our soldiers begin to file out, taking the two Sonny brought with him along.

Sonny looks at me, confused. He grins and begins to rise. I guess he thinks this is over. He's mistaken.

I whip my arm out to grab him by the back of the head, rear back and smash his face into the glass coffee table. He screams, and I'm not sure what's louder, that scream or the sound of his skull cracking the heavy glass surface, but I do it again. A deep line splits the table and blood pools on the glass, dripping over the edge and seeping into the tacky white and gold area rug.

"Nadia is not going to appreciate that, Uncle," Bastian says as I hand Sonny off and adjust my cuffs. Bastian shoves a dazed Sonny against the wall and forces him to look at him. "How would you like twelve men to do to you what they would have done to her?" he asks through gritted teeth, all casualness vanished as his rage surfaces. "We can arrange it."

Sonny reaches into his pocket and produces a switchblade. "You motherfucking half-breeds," he says, and although not quite steady on his feet, he's steady enough to swing the blade toward Bastian's face.

But Bastian's seen it too, and Sonny, still dazed, only manages to nick his jaw before Bastian jerks away. Sonny is slower than he might be otherwise, giving Bastian time to draw his arm back and punch Sonny so hard that he goes down sideways while still gripping the weapon.

"What do you think?" I ask him as I step on his wrist and crouch to take the knife. Bastian sets his knee on Sonny's windpipe. "Do you want to find out what twelve men can do to a woman at their mercy?" he asks, pressing.

"It... wasn't me. I'm telling you," Sonny chokes out. "Her... brother."

Just before Sonny passes out, Bastian shifts his weight off his knee. Sonny gasps for breath. Bastian takes the knife from me and brings it to Sonny's jaw, to the same spot Sonny got him. It's a surface wound, but what he does to Sonny isn't. Sonny's hands fist, and I know it takes all he has not to cry like a fucking baby as blood gushes from his face.

"You crossed a line, Uncle," Bastian says, standing. He drops the switchblade a few feet away.

I stand too, studying Sonny. He holds my gaze as he manages to sit up, his back to the couch. His forehead and the side of his face are already swollen, a bruise forming around his eye, and he's got his hand over the cut Bastian made, but his rage and hate still burn hot in his gaze.

"This was a warning. You stay the fuck away from what is ours." I turn to my brother. "Let's go."

He nods, and we walk to the door.

"Amadeo," Sonny calls out when we get to it. Bastian pulls the door open, and I turn back. "You have many enemies. Watch your back," he says through gritted teeth.

## 8

## VITTORIA

*What happened to you?*

I wake with a start. Bastian's words haunted me throughout a restless sleep. A sleep I couldn't wake from. The nightmare repeated, yet I can't remember anything but the sick feeling it leaves behind. The weight in my stomach. The sweat. The fear. The way it has me turning my hands over again and again searching for something, but I don't know what. And along the edges, when I'd manage to come close to consciousness, were their words. Their question.

*What happened to you?*

I don't know.

Sitting up, I wipe the sweat off my forehead. I search the room, expecting to find one of them here, but it's empty, the light from behind the curtains gone. A glance at the clock tells me it's a little after eight at night. My stomach growls as if realizing just from the time it's missed dinner. I am hungry. Famished.

When the events of the morning replay before my eyes, I push them aside and get up to go into the bathroom. I wash my face and brush my teeth. I study my hands, back and front. They look the same. Not like the hands of a killer. Of a woman who ended the life of a man. But what's frightening isn't that. It's not what I did. It's that I don't feel anything. Not a single thing. What does that make me?

I comb through my hair while I study my reflection. There's a bruise on my forehead along with the cuts that are healing. My body has cuts all over it, but the lingering pain is dull and doesn't bother me.

What would have happened if Amadeo and Bastian hadn't come in time? What would have become of me after those men finished with me? My mind wanders to Emma. Emma is relying on me. She needs me.

With thoughts of my little sister, I walk back into the bedroom and through it to the closet. From inside a shoebox, I get the dagger Amadeo had taken from me that I had taken back. I'd hidden it, not wanting them to find it on me, but if I'd had it when that man had delivered me down to the basement of horrors, maybe things would have gone differently. Maybe they wouldn't have gotten as far as they did.

Standing naked in the closet, I fashion a strap out of a pair of stockings I destroy and tie the dagger to my thigh. No sheath. It's not the smartest thing to do, but I won't be without it again. And I won't let them take it from me. It's not against them that I will use it. Unless they force my hand.

I choose a simple black dress and pair it with high heels. Then I walk back into the bathroom and rummage through the drawers for my makeup bag. From inside it, I find my lipstick. I hate my signature red, yet it's so much a part of me. It fits, I think, that particular shade. The color symbolizes blood and violence. I smear it thick across my lips. I don't bother with anything else but leave the tube open on the counter, not even bothering to pick up the lid when it rolls into the sink. I make my way out into the hallway, half expecting a locked door or a guard but finding myself free.

Walking down the stairs, I'm very aware of the edge of the knife at my thigh. Lights are on in the living and dining rooms. The table is set for three, and I can smell food cooking in the kitchen. I'm about to go in there when the door opens and a woman in a uniform steps through carrying a bowl of salad. She's clearly startled to find me standing there, and I wonder what I look like when it takes her a minute too long to take me in. I look down at the dress, which I think is casual. It's a simple fitted T-shirt dress. But her expression is strange.

"Are Amadeo or Bastian here?" I ask.

"Yes, they're in the study, Mrs. Caballero."

Mrs. Caballero. I'll have to get used to that.

"Thanks," I say, and when she points the way, I

head toward the study. I hear the rumble of their voices as I approach and don't bother to knock before opening the door. The brothers turn when they see me. Amadeo leans against the wall by the window, and Bastian sits on one of the leather chairs. Eyebrows rise and they exchange a glance, and again I'm left wondering what's wrong. I touch my hair, tamp it down. Is it that? Does it look strange? It frizzes and gets huge at a drop of moisture in the air.

"Dandelion," Bastian says, standing. "Nice to see you up and about."

I enter and close the door behind me. "When do we leave for New York?" The sooner we go, the sooner I'm back for Emma, and the sooner this is over. I want nothing more than to be free of all of this. To leave everything behind and go forward.

*Forward to what?*

My throat tightens, and it takes me a minute to collect myself. Amadeo is studying me. He's the more serious of the two. "How do you feel?"

"Can you never ask me that again?" I see the tumbler of whiskey on the desk and pick it up, drinking it all down. I don't actually like whiskey, but I need something tonight. I feel off. Strange.

"You should maybe eat something before you drink, Dandelion," Amadeo says, taking the tumbler from me. My lipstick stains the crystal. He eyes me. "Makeup?"

I shrug a shoulder. "Just lipstick. I always wear it. It makes me feel like myself."

"Does it?" he asks.

Bastian is on his feet now too, and I look between them, remembering the time in the library. My stomach flutters, and I feel my neck and face heat because I want it again. I want to feel them both. I need them both.

"When do we leave?" I ask again, looking slightly over Amadeo's shoulder rather than at him.

"Tonight. Let's go eat dinner." He places a hand on my lower back to guide me out. Bastian follows. We go into the dining room, where Amadeo pulls out a chair, and I sit. They take the seats on either side of me, and the same woman from before comes to serve us.

Tonight's meal is roasted chicken with potatoes, vegetables, and the salad I saw her carrying in. Once we have our dishes, Amadeo pours us each a glass of wine, and I don't wait for them to get started. I pick up my knife and fork and eat, ravenous.

"How is Emma?" I ask as I chew.

"She's fine. She ate dinner about an hour ago, and they're going to make popcorn and watch a movie," Bastian says.

"Good." I shove a huge bite of chicken into my mouth. It's so big that I have to swallow wine to get it down.

"Take it easy." Amadeo lays his hand on mine, and I study his bruised knuckles. It's the hand I'm holding my knife with. Does he know how easily I can stab his? Pin it to the table?

"Dandelion?" he asks. I shift my gaze up and look at him through my lashes. "Everything all right?"

I study his steely eyes. I think about how he watched Bastian fuck me. How he tossed him the lubricant. I think about how he came in my mouth. And I think about how I want it again. It's that sickness in me. All people see is the pretty outside, but inside, I'm rotten. Rotting. Maybe that's why they're looking at me so strangely now. Perhaps they're seeing the real me. They'd be the first.

Tears blur my vision. I shake my head and pick up my wineglass to swallow it all down. "I'm just hungry," I say and continue to devour every bite on my plate. When I'm done, I set down my knife and fork and sit back in my chair to find both brothers watching me closely. I wipe my mouth and wonder what the hell they find so fucking interesting. I remember Bastian's question again. Remember how when I'd said I was tired he'd made the comment that killing will do that to you. I'm a killer. I should feel guilt or remorse or something. Anything.

The kitchen door swings open, and two women emerge to clear our dishes.

"Give us a minute," Amadeo tells them, and they retreat.

"We need to go," I say.

"We have time," Amadeo says as they both stand. "There's something we need to talk about. Let's go into the study."

I look from him to Bastian and back. "What's happened?"

"Come," he says, Bastian moving to the exit as Amadeo pulls my chair out.

"What is it? Tell me."

"Vittoria—"

"Just say it!"

He sighs and shakes his head. "Lucien is filing for guardianship of Emma."

It takes me a minute. "What?"

"Lucien wants to be appointed your sister's legal guardian."

I push my hands into my hair, my head feeling heavy, the food I just scarfed down sitting like a brick in my stomach. I shake my head and look up at them.

"We have her. He can't get to her."

"We kidnapped her."

"But I'm... how can he do that? Why? He doesn't care about her. Certainly doesn't love her."

"It's about leverage," Amadeo says.

"It's not about love. Love doesn't matter," Bastian adds.

I get to my feet, irritated, and go to him. I shove him. "Of course it matters. Love may not matter to someone like you, but it does matter!"

With a snort, he takes my wrists, and I breathe him in. "Someone like me?"

"Yes. Someone like you."

"You're fucked up, Dandelion, you know that?"

"Yeah, I do, Bastian. And guess what? You're just as fucked up. Do *you* know *that*?"

He grins and nods casually. Too casually.

"Is this all a game to both of you?" I ask, turning to face Amadeo when Bastian releases my wrists.

"No game. We have an idea."

I shake my head and step toward the exit of the room. "I want to see my brother."

Amadeo takes my arm and turns me around. He draws me close and searches my face, eyes landing on my mouth and making me remember our last kiss. Making me remember how he gets when we kiss.

But this isn't the time. "Let me go."

He doesn't. Instead, he holds me close as he and his brother share some silent communication.

"Let's go into the study," Bastian says.

"No. There's no time," I say, but Amadeo marches me to the study as Bastian leads the way. Once inside. I'm deposited on the couch. I wince when the blade cuts my thigh and look from one to the other. From the desk, Amadeo retrieves a file.

Dread settles in my stomach when he carries it to me but doesn't quite hand it over.

"Do you remember our conversation from a few nights ago, Dandelion?" Bastian asks, coming to sit beside me. Amadeo takes the seat opposite us.

"Which one?" I rub my temples. I'm getting a headache.

"When I asked you if your mother or father had brown eyes."

"Why does that matter? Lucien will try to take Emma from me." I try to stand, but Bastian puts his hand on my thigh to keep me down. He pauses, then cocks his head to the side and studies me. I watch as he shifts his gaze down to look at his hand. There's a smear of blood across his thumb. He draws the dress up my thigh to reveal the crudely made strap holding the dagger to my thigh. The cuts it's made. The blood.

"What's this, Dandelion?"

The dagger looks like a pretty little toy beside his big hand. I glance up at him, then at Amadeo. Neither look surprised, and I don't feel like apologizing.

"It's mine. I found it in your nightstand after you took it from me," I tell Amadeo. Bastian moves to slip it from my thigh, but I catch his hand with both of mine. "You can't take it away. I won't let you."

"Relax, sweetheart. I just want to have a look."

"Don't call me sweetheart."

"Fine. Dandelion. Relax, Dandelion."

He takes my wrists, drags my arms behind my back and holds them with one of his as he slips the blade from its makeshift sheath. He tests the sharpness against his arm and whistles.

"I'm keeping it. If I'd had it when those men… maybe what happened wouldn't have."

They study me as I try to wriggle free of Bastian's grip to take the dagger back.

"I mean it. I won't be defenseless again."

"We need to bandage the cut and you need a proper strap and sheath for it," Amadeo says as Bastian gets up to go into the attached bathroom. He returns a moment later with a large bandage, then cleans the cuts and covers them with it.

I'm surprised and look from one to the other. They're going to let me keep it? I was sure they'd fight me on it.

Amadeo returns to the desk and opens the center drawer. He drops my knife in it and I'm about to protest when he takes out a switchblade. He pushes the button, and I watch it flip open.

"You can have this one until I get your sheath. It's at the Ravello house." He closes it and offers it to me. Untrusting, I look at him, then at it. I reach to take it expecting him to snatch it away at the last minute, but he doesn't. The handle is smooth, the weight heavy. I push the button and touch the sleek, sharp blade. Holding it open, I look at them.

"You try to use that on either of us, and you'll be back to locked doors and guards, understand?" Amadeo says.

I nod once. It's not for them. Not yet.

"Good. Now about Emma."

I brace myself. This is going to be bad.

"Two blue-eyed parents cannot have a brown-eyed child," Bastian says bluntly.

Amadeo watches me while I try to process.

Bastian's eyebrows rise. "Do you understand what I'm saying?"

I blink, then lower my gaze to my bandaged thigh. For hating me, he takes care of me. It's strange. I touch it, wondering how I didn't really feel it when it cut me with each step, only aware of it almost in my periphery, an aside. I think it's all the things that are happening. They're taking their toll. Snapping that worn-out thread holding me together.

"It's in the file, Vittoria," Amadeo says. When I look at him, I see my reflection in the glass front of the liquor cabinet behind him. I don't look like myself. The shadows under my eyes show how tired I am even though I've slept. But it's not that. There's something deeper. Something broken. Too broken to repair. And I understand why they were all looking at me strangely. The lipstick is almost clown-like, too heavily applied and smeared, stark against my pale skin. With makeup it's fine, but without and given the state I'm in, it just makes me look unhinged. I wipe it away with the back of my hand, managing to smear red across my cheek.

I look at Amadeo. He's watching me intently. Watching me come apart. Because I am unraveling. I feel it.

I set the switchblade aside and climb on top of him, straddling his thighs. I wrap an arm around his neck and pull him to me, kissing him as I slip my other hand between us and undo his belt, the slacks. I slip my hand into his briefs and feel his hardening cock even as he tries to push me off.

"Dandelion," he says against my mouth.

"No." I grip a handful of his short hair. Eyes wide open, I kiss him. And I make him kiss me back. With the other hand, I draw the crotch of my panties aside, rise up on my knees, and slide him inside me with a deep, low moan. "Fuck me. I need you to fuck me."

He groans, kissing me, pulling the dress off me before gripping my hips. I'm not wearing a bra. I didn't bother. He slips one hand into my panties from behind and presses a finger to my other hole. I ride him harder, impaling myself on him again and again, but he draws me off, tearing at the string of my panties and discarding them.

"Fuck me," I tell him, trying to get him inside me again and biting his lips before kissing him, forgetting myself as he pushes his finger into my pussy, lubricating it, then slides it to my back hole.

"I'm fucking your ass," he tells me, gripping both cheeks and forcing them apart.

The leather of a chair creaks, drawing my attention over my shoulder. I turn to find Bastian sitting down, eyes on us. I look back at Amadeo.

"I don't care. Just fuck me. I need you to fuck me," I tell him as he shifts to grip a handful of hair and draws my face to his. With his other hand on my hip, he guides me down, his thick cock at my back entrance. It hurts at first, burns like it did with Bastian, but I need this. I need him inside me with Bastian watching, knowing the pain will morph into something else soon. When Amadeo moans as I take him, I find myself gripping his shoulders and moving my hips, wanting him, my clit rubbing against his stomach as he fucks me while Bastian watches. It's the hottest thing.

"Fuck, Dandelion." Amadeo grips my shoulder,

taking me roughly, and it's moments before I'm coming hard, kissing him, eyes open, lips on lips, my tongue inside his mouth, him devouring it. I ride him hard as he thrusts from beneath me until he stills deep inside me, and we come together. All I can do is hold him. Cling to him. Bury my face in his neck and drown in his essence as I disappear just for a little while.

He draws out of me slowly, watching me. I'm panting, my clit still throbbing. He caresses my hair, his eyes soft as he kisses my cheek, my temple, my ear.

"Take care of Bastian," he tells me, and I glance behind me to find Bastian's dark eyes burning like fire on me, his thick cock in his hand, the head glistening. But my legs are too weak to carry me, so Amadeo hands me to him. Bastian turns me to face him and slides into my pussy. I can't catch my breath as I take him, my too-sensitive clit rubbing against him. He moves from beneath me, holding my face, never closing his eyes as he watches me.

He's so beautiful like this. So raw. And I can't look away.

"I don't know," I tell him, orgasm moments away. "I don't know why I'm like this." I feel a tear slip down my cheek.

"It doesn't matter," he says, leaning in to kiss that tear away, then the next one.

I turn my face to Amadeo and extend one hand to him. He takes it, turns it over, and kisses my wrist.

"I don't know," I say again as I drop my head onto Bastian's shoulder and let my orgasm wash over me. I let it drown me just for a moment. Just this one small, fleeting safe space in time. And when I open my eyes again, I'm lying on my back on the couch with a cushion beneath my head and a blanket over me. I'm dressed. They must have put my dress on me when we were finished. When I passed out.

Amadeo and Bastian are standing at the desk talking quietly, and on the coffee table is the switchblade. The room smells of sex. It's the scent of us. But then my gaze catches on the folder, and I remember our conversation.

My heart feels heavy, but my head is clearer as I sit up. The brothers turn to me. I pick up the folder and open it.

"She's my sister," I tell them, looking over reports I can't really understand. But for the first time since my father's death, I feel like I know what I need to do. The fog has cleared for now at least.

"Half sister. Your father isn't Emma's father, Vittoria," Amadeo says. "You share the same mother but not the same father." I look up at him.

"It doesn't matter. I don't care."

"I know you don't, but it'll work in our favor."

It takes me a minute, but I understand what he means. "Blood."

He nods. "Exactly. If your father isn't her father, it means she shares no blood with Lucien. Which means you can file for custody as her closest blood relation. It gives you the upper hand."

I nod, but I'm thinking. My mother had a lover? I

knew she was unhappy, didn't I? For years. My father was very protective of her to the point of obsession. She was a beautiful bird in a gilded cage. But it was how we were. How he was with both of us. Not with Emma, though. Never with Emma. And things changed at home after she was born. I remember that well. Nothing I could put my finger on, but everything felt different.

"Who is he?" I ask.

"Don't know that yet," Amadeo says.

Bastian comes to sit beside me as I study the bandage on my thigh, tracing the map of bruises and cuts. "We're going to need to bubble wrap you," he says.

I smile, setting my head on his shoulder.

Amadeo sits on the coffee table, his knees touching mine. He tucks a strand of hair behind my ear, and I look up at him. At my beautiful husband. His eyes can look so cold yet hide emotions that burn so hot. I look at his mouth and touch his lips. And I feel my heart slip a little as I sit there with them both.

"You okay, Dandelion?" Amadeo asks.

I wipe away a smear of red on the corner of his mouth. My lipstick. Not blood at least. I nod. "I'm fine." It's a lie. But it doesn't matter if I'm okay or not. Not now. The time for that will come later. After I've taken care of all that I need to take care of. "What do I need to do to file for guardianship?"

# 9

## AMADEO

After flying through the night, we have a few hours to rest and change at our hotel before arriving at the Russo Properties & Holdings building in Manhattan, where the will reading will be held. Bastian and I have been watching Vittoria since the previous evening, but she seems more like the woman she was a few days ago before the attack. Although there is still a glint in her eye, that look that tells me she may be on the side of the abyss now, but she's teetering.

She's dressed in an elegant black Versace midi dress in a lightweight material. It hugs her figure, the bust gathered and collected at the center of her chest by a gold ring. It comes to just below her knees, and she's paired it with patent leather high heels and a gold anklet. Her hair is bound in a neat chignon at the nape of her neck. On her ears are gold studs and on her finger is our wedding band. She left the engagement ring locked in a safe at the house. She's wearing that lipstick again but along with eyeliner and mascara. It looks very different than it did the other night. *She* looks very different. That could also be the sleep she got after another round of fucking on the flight over.

"You look good, Dandelion," I tell her as we ride up to the penthouse.

She meets my gaze, and I get that same sense I've had with her before. Like she's so deep in thought, but when she hears you and looks at you, she's seeing inside you. Nothing is casual with her. No empty words. And I admit she has me hanging on for every last one.

"It's all the fucking," she says, not quietly. "I guess you were right. Everyone wants to come."

One of the two soldiers accompanying us shifts uncomfortably. Bastian chuckles. Bruno pretends to be busy with a text.

Anyone else may have made that comment as a joke but not our Dandelion. She glances from me to Bastian, then straight ahead at her reflection in the mirror, her expression never changing, oblivious to everyone but us.

My brother and I exchange a glance while the soldiers look on as if unseeing, and I wonder if this reprieve, this glimpse of the other, stronger side of her, will last. I have a feeling I know the answer and find myself wanting to be wrong for her sake. Because seeing her as she was, hearing what she said last night, how she didn't know why she was like she is, I don't want that for her. I don't want to see her looking so broken, so damaged anymore. It's enough. I want to fix her.

But I also know this isn't over. She hasn't hit rock bottom yet. And I'm afraid this reading of the will and our meeting with Lucien Russo may pale in comparison to what we learn when we meet with Tilbury.

I wonder if Bastian is thinking the same things because what he warned would happen has happened. My priorities have shifted. My endgame may no longer be the same as his. I wonder what hers is. No, I don't have to wonder. She wants out. She wants to take Emma and walk away. And I promised her I'd let her go, but as the elevator dings and the doors slide open, I'm not sure I can do that anymore. I don't want to.

My first face-to-face meeting with Lucien Russo is not what I expect it to be. I'd imagined I'd be calm. Gleeful, even. Because today brings us another step closer to his end. To justice being served, the scales leveled.

But when Lucien faces his sister as we walk toward him, Bastian and I both move closer to her, standing just a little ahead of her. Enough to protect her from an attack. Not that he would attack here and now, not so openly.

My uncle's words come to mind. That it was Lucien who arranged what happened to her in Naples. Could he have? Or was Sonny fucking with us?

I don't take my eyes off Lucien as he takes her in. He looks like his father but sloppy. Where Geno Russo took care to always look impeccable, Lucien doesn't quite have that same crispness, that natural sense of elegance. He has money, that's easy to see, but there's something ugly and base about him. It's in his eyes—in the flatness, the emptiness of them.

As we approach the room with the glass walls and doors, we're met with one of Geno Russo's lawyers, John Brady. Bruno shakes hands with him, and I guess he's one of the lawyers he's been in contact with to arrange things. We're introduced to the other two. Vittoria shakes their hands. My brother and I merely nod in acknowledgment as Lucien shifts his gaze from his sister to us.

Bastian's disdainful gaze sweeps over him. "Been a few years, Russo."

Lucien's eyes narrow. He's shorter than us by several inches. Older. Softer. "You never did know when to keep your mouth shut," Lucien says. I guess he's still the biggest asshole in the room.

Vittoria wraps a hand around the fist Bastian makes. "Lucien," she says calmly.

Lucien's eyes move to her hands, first the one curled around Bastian's, then the one with the wedding band, then to me.

"I'm confused. Who the fuck is who?"

Brady clears his throat. He's the oldest of the attorneys present, and I guess he's not used to that type of language.

"This is my husband, Amadeo, and his brother, Bastian."

Lucien rolls his eyes. "It was rhetorical, sis."

She studies him in that way she has that can set anyone on edge, and Lucien is not immune.

Bruno introduces himself to the other lawyers.

"Why don't we get on with the reading of the will?" I suggest. "We have more appointments while we're in town."

Brady clears his throat. "I'm afraid your brother-in-law will not be able to enter with us. Family only. And of course, your attorney," he says to Vittoria.

"I give him permission," she says.

"I'm afraid it doesn't work that way, sis," Lucien says.

She opens her mouth to protest, but Brady clears his throat. "However, I'm told we'll have some other business after the reading of your father's will," he says, glancing at Bruno and then at Bastian. "If you could please remain close."

Bastian gives him an irritated nod and makes a show of sitting on the couch in the waiting area.

Lucien grins. A small victory for him. We enter the room and take our seats around the large oval table with Lucien and his lawyers on one side, and Vittoria, Bruno, and I on the other.

While Brady gets on with the reading of Geno Russo's will, I study Lucien Russo. I look at the ring with the family's insignia on his finger. I remember it from that day in our kitchen. Remember the toe of his shiny, expensive shoes when he stepped on the money his father had scattered on that shitty linoleum floor. I think of his hands on Hannah. Sweet, young, innocent Hannah. Helpless Hannah.

My hands fist. I sit up and lean my forearms on the table. Brady passes a sealed letter to Vittoria and another to Lucien. Vittoria traces her name on hers. It's handwritten. Lucien jams his into his pocket, leaving me to wonder if he'll bother to read it at all.

Brady finally gets down to it.

Lucien, already owning thirty shares of the company, will inherit nineteen more of his father's shares, putting him at forty-nine percent. Lucien opens his mouth, clearly surprised.

"When did he change it?" he demands, cutting Brady off.

"We'll get to questions." Brady's unruffled by Lucien's tone and carries on reading. He explains how Vittoria will come into her thirty shares on her twenty-first birthday and will inherit twenty-one more on that same day.

"What?" Vittoria asks. She too is surprised. As surprised as me.

I watch them, glance at my brother through the glass wall. We expected the shares would be split fifty-fifty, knowing he wouldn't leave anything to Emma, but this is a surprise. And makes my job a hell of a lot easier.

Lucien's hands are fists. "When did he fucking change the will? He wasn't in his right mind the last few months, I can tell you that. He was slipping. If he—"

"The change was made nearly seven years ago, Mr. Russo."

Lucien's face pales as he's momentarily dumbstruck. I wonder if anyone else notices it. Notices how his shifty eyes move over his sister.

"And there is no contesting it on grounds that your father was not in his right mind," Brady says firmly. I tune him out as he continues reading more details.

Her father changed his will seven years ago. I look at Vittoria. Is she doing the math? She would have been fourteen. The timing coincides with the year she lost. The question is why Geno Russo did it. Why he gave Vittoria controlling shares of his business.

I turn to Lucien. See the sweat on his brow as he texts something with his thick thumbs as he curses. He moves to stand, and I see the corner of the letter he pushed carelessly into his pocket. See the one Vittoria is still holding with reverence.

Did Geno Russo change his will to punish his son? He'd have to know it would put Vittoria in danger, but she was already in danger. A fifty-fifty split would give them equal power. If anything would have happened to her, the shares would shift to him because the company must be controlled by the family. This much I already knew. It was her father's wish. In fact, if anything happens before those shares are transferred on her twenty-first birthday, everything will still go to Lucien. After she's twenty-one, should anything happen to Vittoria, those shares would remain mine as her husband. It's why I married her. Why we had to do things the way we did.

"Do you have any questions, Ms. Russo? Excuse me, Mrs. Caballero. I realize this may come as a shock, but you own controlling shares of the company."

"I don't..." She shakes her head. "What about my sister? You haven't mentioned Emma."

Lucien snorts.

"Emma is not accounted for in the will," Mr. Brady says, clearly uncomfortable. "Your father was very clear in his instruction regarding your younger sister." He pauses politely. "That concludes this meeting, but my office will set up a time to go over everything with you in greater detail and handle the transfer of shares on your twenty-first birthday which is coming up, young lady," he says with a smile. Vittoria attempts to smile but falls short. He glances back at Lucien, who is staring out the window as he whisper-shouts into his phone. "You should know that your father was very proud of you, Vittoria," he says to her and pats her hand.

Vittoria's eyes water, and I think about how she felt about him. How she loved him. But I clear my throat. Time to get on with the business of things.

"Excellent," I say just to get on with things. "Thank you, Mr. Brady. And now that that's done and given that I am in control of Vittoria's finances, which thus includes her shares of the company, I'd like to request an audit to be conducted immediately. I'd like to know exactly what my wife and I are getting into."

Brady looks at me. He doesn't trust me. I get it. I wouldn't trust me either. "That's premature, don't you—"

"You what?" Lucien starts, turning back to us, the look in his eyes that of pure hate as they move over me and settle on his sister.

I smile and stand, buttoning my jacket as I pull Vittoria's chair out. "My attorney has all the paperwork. I'm sure it's in order. If you'll excuse us, it's been a long day. My wife and I are tired. Vittoria."

Vittoria tucks the letter into her bag, looks up at me, then back at her brother. She stands. "I'd like a private moment with my brother," she says.

The lawyers nod and start to pack up, Brady saying something about coffee.

Setting a hand on her shoulder, I squeeze, then lean down so my mouth is at her ear. "What are you doing?"

She looks up at me. "You and Bastian have your agenda, and I've given you everything you asked for. This is mine," she says and stands, her eyes over my shoulder on her brother.

I set my hand on her waist as everyone begins to file out. "I don't want you alone with him."

She drags her gaze to me, and I have her full attention. "He won't hurt me. He's too much a coward to touch me," she says so only I hear.

"Vittoria."

She brushes something off my shoulder. "Besides,

you and Bastian are right outside the glass wall. You can see everything."

"Mr. Caballero?" Brady says from the door.

I glance at him, then at my wife. "I don't like this."

"You don't have to."

## 10

## VITTORIA

The door clicks closed. Lucien's eyes move to it, but mine remain locked on him. In my hand, I clutch my bag containing the letter my father wrote me and wait for him to look at me.

"Which one are you fucking?"

"Both."

He's clearly not expecting honesty but recovers himself quickly and snorts. "Guess it stuck."

I am momentarily confused but get to the point. "Did you do what they said?"

His eyes are shifty. "What did they say, dear sister?"

I look up at him, at my half brother whom I don't know. I certainly don't like or trust him. But could he have done what they've accused him of? Is he that much of a monster?

"Their sister," I say more quietly, not sure I want to know the answer.

His eyebrows rise. "What did they say I did to her?"

"She was fourteen. You were an adult. They said you raped her."

He shakes his head and looks away momentarily. "She was young, I get that now, but I didn't rape her. We were in love."

I'm shocked at his answer. Struck silent for a long moment. "She was fourteen," I finally say. "You were what? Nineteen? Twenty?" Does he really believe they were in love?

He pushes a hand through his hair, his face growing red.

"Do you really believe that you were in love?" I ask.

He ignores my question and asks another. "You signed away control of your fucking finances? Are you that stupid?"

"I had no choice. Not when you left me in Italy to fend for myself. Did you even try to send anyone after me?"

His right eye twitches. It's an infinitesimal movement, but I've learned to watch my brother closely over the years, and I know what this means. He's angry because he feels himself losing control. He got that look with dad often when it came to finances or the business.

"You shouldn't have gone. I told you that."

"Our father's last wish was that he be buried in Italian soil where his roots are. It was his dream to go back home one day, you know that."

"I don't think he dreamt of going in a fucking box. What did you sign exactly? We can get you out of it, get the marriage annulled. They're holding you against your will. It's not the fucking dark ages, for fuck's sake."

"I don't care about the money."

His eyebrows disappear into his receding hairline. Dad had a full head of hair. He clearly did not pass that gene down to my bother.

"You'd better learn to care if you'd like to see Emma again. I'm taking guardianship of her."

"You're not. You can't. You're not even blood."

"Ah! Your eyes are opening. Finally. Your mother was unfaithful, Vittoria." He spits the word unfaithful. "And she was punished."

"What do you mean?"

"I'm trying to help you."

"This is you helping me?"

"Were you in on the kidnapping? There is video footage. In fact, that one there"—he gestures beyond the glass wall—"will be arrested…" He pauses, checks his watch. "In about three minutes."

"What?" Panic has me turning to look at Bastian and Amadeo, who, although in conversation with Bruno, are watching us intently.

He grins, cocks his head, and looks me over as if seeing me for the first time. "There is video footage of him kidnapping Emma and the idiot nanny. Of his men knocking that shrink out. Do you even know who the fuck you've gotten yourself tangled up with, Vittoria?"

"You can't have him arrested." I need to warn Bastian, but Lucien grabs my arm.

"What did you sign?"

"Let me go. Do you even care why we're here? That our father is dead?"

He seems surprised by the question. Like it's an odd thing to ask. The elevator dings, and I half turn.

"There they are," Lucien says, tugging me close as Bastian and Amadeo's attention turns to the elevator. "You didn't know him like I did, Vittoria. Our father was a cruel man. You don't know the things he did. What he was capable of."

"He wasn't like that."

"Do you ever wonder about his reaction when your mom was killed? How he didn't really seem all that surprised or upset. Well, I mean, he was surprised that little Emma made it, I guess. But don't you wonder?"

"Get off me!"

"Ah." He smiles, holds me tight but turns me so we watch together as a dozen men in SWAT gear rush in with their weapons ready and have the few soldiers Amadeo and Bastian brought on the ground in minutes. They slam Bastian against one wall and Amadeo against another.

"Stop!" I call out, trying to free myself of my brother but unable. I watch powerlessly. I can't hear a sound through the solid glass wall. Amadeo fights for his brother, Bruno is held back, the soldiers kept down while Brady and the other lawyers stand back and watch as if they knew all along. Bastian is handcuffed and forced toward the elevator by two men as two others hold Amadeo back.

Lucien tugs me toward him, making me face him. "You know people are killed in custody all the time. Accidents happen more often than you'd think." He laughs a strange laugh, something that sends a chill down my spine. An image slices through my skull, a shudder of memory, of sight and sound. That laugh. That terrible laugh.

My knees buckle, and I grab the back of the chair nearest me. I remember when Amadeo asked me what seems like a lifetime ago if I was afraid of my brother. I'd told him I wasn't. But it wasn't true, not really. I always knew our father would protect me from Lucien. But it's not that I wasn't afraid of Lucien.

"Let go of her!"

The door slams against the wall so hard it jerks me out of my thoughts. I blink, look up at Lucien who is grinning down at me, his grip so tight on my arm I know I'll have another bruise to add to the collection.

"You don't deserve my help, you know that?" he asks, any enjoyment vanishing. When Amadeo is close enough, Lucien shoves me to him and backs away, clearly afraid of Amadeo.

"He's going to kill Bastian," I tell Amadeo frantically. He catches me and holds on to me as our soldiers rush in along with the lawyers. I turn into Amadeo's arms and press myself to him. He looks down at me, pushing hair that's fallen out of my chignon back from my face. "Lucien is going to kill him."

Amadeo tries to push me aside to advance on Lucien. I hug my arms around him because I see the look in his eyes. I see how dangerous his rage is. If he gets near Lucien, he'll kill him. He will beat him to death with his bare fists, and I'll lose him, too. The police will arrest him too.

I clutch at his face with both hands to make him look at me. "We need to go. We need to get to Bastian!" It's taking all my strength to just slow him down. "Amadeo. Please. Look at me. I need you. I need you!"

That gets his attention, but I know it's momentary because the control of earlier is gone, and even then, it was barely there. I felt the rigidity of his body beside mine as the will was read. I saw how his hands fisted and what it took for him to maintain control.

"Take me away. Please. Take me away from here. I need you."

## 11

## AMADEO

What the fuck just happened? What the fuck did Lucien Russo just manage to pull off?

I look down at Vittoria. She's frantic, tugging at my hair and face to get my attention.

"I need you," she keeps saying. "Please, Amadeo. I need you."

I blink, forcing myself to focus on her face. Her hair has come out of its chignon. Her cheeks are flushed with the exertion of getting my attention. Of getting away from her brother. I wrap one arm around her waist and nod. I turn to find Lucien Russo with his tail between his legs, scurrying out the door to the elevators, flanked by two men in SWAT gear. He took advantage of my distraction because he has just declared outright war.

"What the fuck just happened?" I demand of Bruno.

Bruno rushes in as he disconnects one call to answer another.

"He's going to kill him," Vittoria says, her eyes red and watery. "He said accidents happen. He said—"

"Those weren't cops. They were soldiers," I tell Bruno when he disconnects.

He shakes his head, caught off guard and rattled. "Shit."

"We need to find out where they're taking him."

He nods, his attention in his phone as he types back a reply to a text. "The car tailing them lost them."

Fuck!

"Take her," I say, digging my phone out of my pocket as I hand Vittoria to him.

"No!" she cries, clinging to me.

"Get her to one of the SUVs. You ride with her. I want two soldiers in the vehicle with you, and you two follow with a second car. You're with her at all times. Am I clear?"

The soldiers nod.

"Amadeo, you'll be on your own," Bruno says. "This isn't our city."

No fucking shit. "I'm calling in a favor. Get her out of here. Do not go back to the hotel. I'll send you an address as soon as I can."

"Amadeo!" Vittoria breaks away from Bruno and runs to me. I'm surprised by the force of her hurling herself into my arms. "I want to stay with you. We need to get him out of there. We need—"

"I *need* to make a call. And you *need* to go with Bruno. Now. Do you understand?"

"He's going to—"

I shake her. "Dandelion. Now!" I gesture to a soldier who takes her and turn my back so I don't have to see her struggle against him as he drags her away. I hit the call button on a number I've never used. One my grandfather passed along.

Favors are carried down from generation to generation. And my grandfather had helped Franco Benedetti when he ran this city. Franco's dead now and has been for years, but this successor will answer this call.

"Who is this?" says the man who picks up on the second ring.

"Amadeo Caballero, Humberto Caballero's grandson. I need Dominic Benedetti."

A long silence follows, then footsteps.

"Amadeo. This is Dominic Benedetti. How can I help you?"

---

I TEXT THE ADDRESS OF THE PENTHOUSE TO BRUNO AND make my way down on the elevator. Just as I step out of the building and head toward the last SUV with its lone driver, four more SUVs pull up. Dominic works fast. One circles around ahead of us, and my driver follows while the other three tail us.

Those men weren't cops or any arm of any legal establishment. They were Lucien Russo's men. Or at least men Russo most likely borrowed from one of his associates. It was done to distract us. To separate us. He couldn't kill us outright. Not so publicly.

Vittoria's panicked words repeat in my head, her worried face swimming before my eyes.

*They're going to kill him.*

They're going to try. I know that.

I grit my teeth. At least Dominic with all this contacts in the city was able to learn where the entourage was headed. We ride fast to the location my brother has been taken to. I don't let myself think about being too late. I can't.

Over an hour later as we slow to enter the lot of the abandoned meat processing plant, I get a text from Dominic telling me to stay put. I watch as men dressed much like those who filed into the top floor of Russo Properties & Holdings to take my brother stalk close to the wall toward two separate entrances.

I don't want to stay put. I want to be there. I want to put a fucking bullet into every one of the bastards who grabbed my brother.

I take my gun out of its holster and climb out of the vehicle. My driver does the same. Neither of us is wearing protective gear while Dominic's men came dressed for war.

On the command of the one in charge, the men stream into the building. I expect to hear gunfire, but it's quiet. I hurry toward the entrance and see why. Lucien's men are easily outnumbered and clearly taken by surprise. Their weapons are not ready and gear is discarded as they sit laughing and talking in a language I don't understand, but it sounds Eastern European mixed with Russian. Vests with SWAT typed out on them lie haphazard on the floor. This is not an organized operation.

Dominic's men round them up, only two shots fired with silencers in place as others are knocked to the ground and driven to their knees.

I don't see Bastian anywhere, though, and look around, circling behind abandoned machinery to where I hear more men. Laughter. And my brother telling someone to go fuck himself. I hurry toward the sound, Dominic's men at my back, and see them in a wide open room with drains along the cracked tile floor. Meat hooks dangle from the ceiling. My brother hangs from one, handcuffs hooked, and his hands holding tight to support his weight. He's shirtless and barefoot. His feet don't touch the ground. And from here, I can see the damage they've done to his chest. His back.

A man gears up to punch him in the gut. Bastian grunts as the man turns to his buddies and laughs. But he doesn't know my brother. Bastian lays his weight into the swing, using momentum, and lifts his legs as he swings back toward the asshole who hit him. He manages to kick him in the face when he turns around.

The man curses, then spits blood. His friends laugh outright, but he reaches for a cattle prod. I have my gun out, and before he can get close to Bastian, I shoot the bastard in the side of the head. Blood splatters my brother as the man stands momentarily still, as if his body hasn't registered the fact that he just died, before he falls over sideways.

It takes his buddies a moment to process what has just happened, and by the time they get their weapons, Dominic's men are on them.

"Don't kill them outright," I order as I hurry to Bastian.

"Took you fucking long enough, brother," Bastian says as I lift him just high enough so he can get his arms free of the hook. I set him down, see him wince, and wonder what damage they did to the bottoms of his feet. His wrists are raw and bloody, burns and bruises mark his chest, stomach, shoulders, and back. But he stands straighter, swallowing down the pain. "Give me your gun."

I hand it over, taking in the bruise around his eye and the cut along his lip. And I watch as, rather than using the gun to shoot his tormentors, he beats the shit out of each one with the butt of the pistol, wrists still cuffed, until six men are lying barely conscious on the filthy ground.

He crouches down beside the body of the one I shot and digs into his pockets to retrieve the key to the cuffs. He stands and holds it out to me. I can see he's in pain.

"You okay?" I ask.

"I'll be fine. Vittoria?"

"Safehouse."

"Good." He looks at the men as I unlock his cuffs.

"Hang them from the meat hooks. Wait until they come around to kill them," I tell Dominic's soldiers.

"And do it slow," Bastian adds. He wipes blood from the corner of his mouth and turns his back on the scene. I can see he's rattled. But more than that, he's pissed.

"Lucien Russo is mine," he says.

"He's yours."

## 12

## VITTORIA

I pace the penthouse, my mind whirling. What just happened? How did things go sideways so quickly? I perch on the edge of the leather chesterfield of this very modern, masculine space and set my head in my hands. It's pounding. I look out the window at the busy street below, but we're too far up for me to recognize any of the hundreds of SUVs that pass.

Bruno is also pacing. He's as worried as me, and I realize how strange this is. How he and I are both concerned about the brothers. Days ago, would I have cared at all?

I get up, discarding my heels on the Persian rug and crossing the room to the bathroom where I search the cabinet for aspirin. I find some and take two with a handful of water from the tap. I splash water on my face and pat it dry when I finally hear them in the other room. I rush out to find Bastian and Amadeo walking into the penthouse, Amadeo carrying some of Bastian's weight and both looking like they've been through hell. Bastian especially. He's barefoot, shirtless, and I gasp, covering my mouth with my hand when I see how his chest is covered in strange bruises, bloody circles.

They stop when they see me. I drag my gaze to Bastian's face to take in the bruise around one eye and the cut on his lip, then look at Amadeo and see the blood on him. It's not his blood at least.

Bastian was tortured. Lucien did this. Lucien ordered this to be done. How? How did he gain so much power? And who are the men who carried out the false arrest in front of our eyes? The torture that followed. Because when my father was alive, they may have had dealings with local crime families, but Lucien never had men like those at his command.

Bruno is talking to them, something about a doctor being on his way. I walk toward the brothers. On the one hand, I'm relieved, but on the other, I don't know. How could this happen? How could Lucien attack them so openly?

"Dandelion," Bastian says. "Don't tell me you were worried about me."

I want to have some smart retort—something clever to say—because I shouldn't care. But I do. And I find at that moment, all I can do is try to manage this swell of emotions because there's no reason for me to be crying. Yet here I am, standing in the middle of a stranger's house crying for the men who kidnapped me, who forced me into a marriage with one. Who had me sign away my inheritance and used my love for my sister to get what they wanted.

But who also took care of me when I was attacked. Who risked everything to bring my little sister to me and get her away from a man who I know now is more monster than human.

"Is it that bad?" Bastian asks Amadeo, his tone light, but I notice how he winces as he shifts from one foot to the other. I know what effort just standing here and trying to make light of this is taking him.

"You have looked better," Amadeo says.

"I'll always look better than you, brother," Bastian tells him with a pat on the back. I think this banter is for my benefit. And there's that feeling again. That strange skipping of my heart.

"Doctor's here," Bruno says, and we all turn to find a short, middle-aged man carrying a medical bag escorted in by two soldiers. Dominic Benedetti's men, according to Bruno. He's the head of the ruling family here and the man who helped Amadeo find Bastian as quickly as he did. Beside him is a woman in a nurse's uniform.

"Mr. Benedetti sent me," the man says and introduces himself as Dr. Lawler. He looks at Bastian. "Let's go into one of the bedrooms. This way."

He very clearly knows the layout of things, so we follow him.

"Vittoria," Bruno calls.

I turn.

"Let's go over a couple of things in your filing for guardianship of Emma while the doctor looks Bastian over."

"I want to be there."

"It's probably best you're not. Let him work."

Amadeo closes the bedroom door without a glance at me, and I stand staring at that closed door for a moment feeling left out. Hurt, if I'm honest.

"Vittoria?" Bruno calls.

I turn to him. I need to remember who I am then. Remember it was my brother who ordered the attack. Of course they don't want me near them.

I follow Bruno into the dining room. It has impressive views from the large floor-to-ceiling window, but all I see is that closed door as Bruno takes out the paperwork and goes over it with me, telling me where to sign and what it all means even as I half-listen, trying to work out where I stand. What I want. What it is I'm feeling.

Once Bruno and I are finished, I find myself back in the living room on the couch looking out over what is turning into a cloudy, wet evening. I lean back and draw my knees up then remember the letter Mr. Brady had given me. My purse is on the coffee table, and I lean to get it and take out the letter. I'm alone in the living room, Bruno busy on yet another call, and both Dominic Benedetti's and Amadeo's soldiers ignore me as they keep watch. But this penthouse belongs to Dominic Benedetti. Lucien wouldn't attack here because he'd not only be attacking Amadeo and Bastian, but he'd be declaring war on the man who controls the city. The thugs he deals with, the ones I know of, at least, are lower-level foot soldiers in various organizations, and even if they don't bow to Benedetti, going against him would mean a death sentence.

I shift in my seat and hold the envelope in my hand. I trace my name written in my father's neat handwriting. I realize as if for the first time that I will never see him again. I will never hear his voice again. Never hug him again.

I slip my finger beneath the flap and unseal it, and I swear I catch a hint of the cologne he wore every day since I can remember. It's probably my imagination but I don't care as I slip the pages out, unfold them and begin to read.

*My dearest Vittoria,*

*It's taken me a long time to sit down and write this letter to you because I know you will only read it once I've passed, and the fact that I'll be leaving you alone in this world is too painful a thought.*

*You have been the light of my life. The bringer of joy. My only source of constant and bright sunshine. Where everyone else has betrayed me, you have been constant. And in our case, it is I who failed you when you needed me most.*

*By now, Mr. Brady has read my will, and you will know that you inherit controlling shares of Russo Properties & Holdings. Your brother knows the reason behind his punishment. But he does not matter. It is you who matters.*

*Ask Brady to arrange security for you if you don't*

*already have round-the-clock bodyguards. I can imagine how Lucien may react to the news that he must now bend a knee to his half sister. Do not underestimate your brother. I have tied his hands as best I can, but given the bylaws, I could only do so much. Just remember to take care. He may hurt you again if he has the chance.*

*I hope you know how much I love you. I hope you know everything I did I did to save you. And always remember, my princess, that what doesn't kill you makes you stronger. You are the strongest woman I know. You survived events that would have destroyed anyone else. You ended those who dared lay a hand on you, and you are a force to be reckoned with.*

*Remember this always. And please try to remember me always as you knew me.*

*I love you so very much.*

*Daddy*

I re-read the letter, both emotional and confused by it. What did Lucien do that he punished him so harshly? What did Mr. Brady say about when my father had changed the will? Almost seven years ago? And the part about me ending those who dared lay a hand on me. It makes no sense. The comment about everyone betraying him I can understand. I think he means Mom. He knew Emma wasn't his or at last must have suspected and, if I know him, confirmed by a DNA test. It's easy enough to do with no one being the wiser.

I read my father's last words to try and remember him as I knew him. He had a reputation for being ruthless in business. He was ruthless with Lucien. I'd heard him speak with staff in a way that made me cringe but with me, he was only kind and good. The way those words are written is strange. He chose them with care, I can see that. Why? Why leave me this letter at all? It only raises questions.

Lucien's words play in my mind.

*"Do you ever wonder about his reaction when your mom was killed? How he didn't really seem all that surprised or upset. Well, I mean, he was surprised that little Emma made it, I guess. But don't you wonder?"*

I shudder at the implication and set the letter aside. I'm tired, jet-lagged, and just exhausted from all that's happened. But I'm too wound up to sleep. I stand and go to the liquor cabinet across the room. I look through it, choose something strong, a whiskey. I pour a healthy serving and drink it all, needing it to warm me up. Needing it to soften body and mind. I pour another and carry the bottle back to the couch to re-read the letter yet again as rain begins to ping against the floor-to-ceiling window. I switch on a lamp as darkness falls and lay my head on the arm of the sofa to watch the storm until my eyelids grow too heavy, and I let myself drift to sleep.

## 13

## BASTIAN

Most of my injuries are on the surface apart from the burns on the bottoms of my feet, which hurt like a motherfucker. A couple of ribs are bruised. The prod left burn marks, and although I'll walk away with a few scars, I will walk away.

I refused the heavier painkillers because they'll trap me in sleep. But what the doctor shot me with is making me drift in and out anyway. Amadeo and Bruno are talking quietly. I pick up bits and pieces of conversation as I move in and out of consciousness so reality and dream intermingle. But when the scene in the kitchen comes into focus, I know I'm moving into unconscious almost right away. I know it every single time. The nightmare has played this opening scene for fifteen years. Yet it never fails to bring me to my knees. Here, in this kitchen, I'm not yet a man. I'm a helpless, stupid boy. A boy whose words sentence his family to their fate.

Tonight, though, it's a little different. Tonight, Geno Russo is a blur. Lucien is center stage, looking like he did earlier in the day. And the soldier who cuts my face is the man with the cattle prod.

*"You never did know when to keep your mouth shut,"* Lucien says.

And then it plays out exactly as it always does. My mother screaming. The bat coming down on my father's knees. The blade slicing Amadeo's face. My face.

God. Fuck. I can feel it like it's real, and I know I'm fucking dreaming it. I know. But by the time I can drag myself out, by the time I open my eyes and bolt upright, I'm covered in sweat.

I take a minute to catch my breath. To look around and know that I'm alone in the bedroom. The curtains are drawn, and it's dark.

We're in one of Dominic Benedetti's penthouses in the city. Not a safehouse per se, but safe all the same because no one would be stupid enough to attack us while we're under his roof. Lucien Russo doesn't have that kind of manpower. He's borrowing it. That much Bruno learned. As much as Lucien Russo wants to be the big man on campus, he's nothing. He has no soldiers of his own. He hires mercenaries and the problem with mercenaries is their loyalties are fluid at best. They're always willing to change sides if the terms are better. The guards he'd sent to protect Vittoria during their father's funeral were easy enough to buy off. None of the men who work for him or those he borrows would lay down their own lives for him.

According to Bruno, these particular soldiers were hired from a local crime organization that typically operates outside of Benedetti territory. One he's already in debt to. They're now down a dozen men. I'm guessing that's going to cost Lucien.

I push the blanket aside, my entire body a dull ache. But the true pain only comes when I put my bandaged feet on the floor and stand. I suck in a breath as I make my way across the room to the bathroom. I need to piss. When I'm back in the bedroom, I'm no longer alone.

"Dandelion."

Vittoria is standing beside the door. She's in her bra and panties, which is surprising, considering the soldiers around the penthouse. Her makeup has long since worn off and her hair is stuck to her forehead like it's wet. She's also barefoot and just looks out of sorts. A little lost.

"Where are your clothes?" I ask.

She looks down as if just realizing she's not quite dressed. "I was sleeping."

"Hm." I pad across the room and get back into bed. I'm tempted to take the pills the doctor left, but I know they'll knock me out, and I don't want that. But just beneath the glass of water is a folded piece of paper. I take it, recognizing my brother's handwriting.

*Bruno and I are going to see Tilbury. Get some rest. I'll let you know what we find.*

I glance at Vittoria and crumple the note. Amadeo and I were supposed to go together, but given what's happened, I get it. I'd be hobbling along, and Vittoria would be left on her own. Even given the soldiers, one of us needs to stay with her.

"You're creeping me out a little standing there like a ghost," I say as I drop the note into the drawer and sit back against the headboard.

"I'm not a ghost," she says and walks over to the bed. I notice she's teetering a little, and when she raises her arm, and I see the bottle of whiskey, I can guess why. "Amadeo said you're not taking the painkillers, so I brought whiskey."

"Good girl." I take the whiskey and drink straight from the bottle.

She walks around the bed, lifts the covers, and climbs in to sit beside me. She takes the bottle and drinks from it, then hands it back.

"You okay there, Dandelion?" She looks odd. Like she's already had some whiskey, for starters, and I'm not sure she can handle a whole lot of it. But more than that, it's that strange look she gets in her eyes, and it's coupled with a distance I don't like. Crazy I can handle. And she is fucking crazy. But that distance is unreachable.

"I heard you curse," she says.

So I wasn't quiet. I take in the dampness at her

hairline and realize her hair isn't wet. It's stuck to sweat.

"I woke you up," I say.

She shrugs a shoulder. "I didn't want to sleep anyway."

"Nightmare?"

She bites her lip. "Yes."

"They're just dreams, you know. Not real."

She looks at me curiously. "Does that work for you?"

It's my turn to shrug my shoulder.

"Are you okay?" she asks.

"I'll be fine. The assholes who did this won't. You should get some sleep."

"That's what Amadeo said." She reaches out a hand to touch a bruise on my lower ribs. "Can I stay with you?"

"Don't want to sleep alone?"

She shakes her head.

"When did he leave?"

"I'm not sure. He went to bed with me, but that was a few hours ago, and he's gone. Bruno too. It's just the soldiers."

"And you're giving them a show in your underwear." I take a sip from the bottle.

"I just walked down the hall to come here. Nobody looked at me."

"They looked, trust me. Don't prance around like this in front of them, understand?"

"I wasn't prancing, and besides, I don't care about

them." She takes the bottle from me and sips. "Do you know where he went?"

"Just running an errand."

"What errand?"

"Nothing you need to worry about."

"Does it have to do with my brother?"

"No."

She looks at me like she doesn't quite believe me but decides not to pursue it.

"How much did you drink?" I ask.

"A little." She lies down and turns on her side toward me.

"More than a little I think." I lie down on my back, and she curls into me. I wince when she lays her head on my chest but again swallow down the pain and wrap an arm around her. "What time is it?"

"Three in the morning."

It's late. I pick up my phone from the nightstand to see if Amadeo's texted but nothing. I send him a text.

Me: *How is the good doctor?*

The three little dots begin to undulate as my brother types, and the relief I feel surprises me. Lucien's attack rattled me. Not for what they did to me, but for the fact that he got to us so easily, and I guess I'm more worried than I realize.

Amadeo: *Don't know yet but my gut says this is going to be bad. Dandelion sleeping?*

Me: *She just crawled into my bed.*

Amadeo: *Keep her there.*

I glance down at the top of Vittoria's head. Her breathing is even. I wonder if she fell asleep.

I set the phone aside and hug Vittoria closer.

"Where did he go?" she asks without moving.

"Nowhere, Dandelion. Get some sleep."

"Are you going to be here when I wake up?"

"I'm not going anywhere, sweetheart."

She curls up tighter, and I think she's going to sleep, but a few minutes later, she asks me another question. "Do you remember them?"

"What?"

"The nightmares."

"Yeah, I do. Wish I didn't."

"No, you don't." She looks up at me. "I can't remember mine, but it's the same one."

"If you can't remember them, then how do you know it's the same one?"

"There's a feeling with it. Like I'm going to be sick."

I study her, thrown off. But before I can say anything, she speaks again.

"It's my birthday."

"Oh yeah. I guess it is. Happy birthday."

"Do you think Lucien will go away now? I'll sign everything later today, and it'll be over. He can't get anything, even if he kills me. It all goes to Amadeo."

"Christ." I draw back and look down at her. She shifts her gaze up to mine. "He's not going to get anywhere near you. We won't let that happen." I hear myself say it, and there's a part of me that wonders when things got to where they got. When the endgame shifted.

She doesn't speak for a long time, but I can almost hear her thinking, trying to sort through things. "Do you think my mother's car accident wasn't an accident?"

"You know whiskey and thinking in the middle of the night aren't always the best combination."

"It's not the whiskey."

"Get some sleep, Dandelion. You're tired and a little drunk."

"What do you think?"

"Why is this coming up now?"

"Lucien said something to me back in the office before those men came. He asked if I noticed Dad's reaction to the news that Mom had been killed. That he wasn't surprised or upset."

"Your brother is an asshole who wanted a reaction out of you. He just found out that you have control of the company he expected to run. He wanted to upset you, and he did. Don't let him win."

She sits up, looks down at me, and lets her gaze sweep over me before she meets mine again. "He won't win. I won't let him. But that's not what I asked you."

I reach up and tug her long blond hair. "Get some rest. You can call Emma when you wake up. FaceTime with her. But if you look like a ghost, you'll just scare the poor kid."

"Just tell me what you think. I know you think something."

I turn away. "Well, if you already know, then there's no point in asking, is there?"

She puts her hand on my shoulder, and I stiffen as she traces the bandage over one of the worst burns.

"Does it hurt?" she asks, pressing on it a little.

I roll back and snatch her wrist. "What the fuck is wrong with you?"

"I just want to know what you know. Is that too much to ask?"

I sit up, shift my weight so I straddle her thighs, and take hold of her free wrist. I look down at her breasts and the tiny scrap of a bra. "What I know, Dandelion, is that it's very hard for me to have you in my bed and not fuck you."

She studies me curiously. "But you won't touch me without Amadeo here."

I shake my head. "No. Out of respect for my brother."

Her gaze shifts to my lips, then lower to my dick pressing against my briefs. I tilt my head and raise an eyebrow. I'm hard.

"Do you wonder why we're like this?" she asks, looking up at me. "All of us, I mean. Fucked up like this. Sleeping with the enemy and wanting it."

I smile, then shift my weight off her. "You are quite the philosopher tonight. But I'm tired. You do what you want. I'm going to sleep." I lie down on my back, and she immediately straddles me, rubbing herself against my cock through her panties and my briefs.

"I want to come." She slips her hand into her

panties, and I watch, unable not to, as she applies herself to the task.

Fuck. Fuck me hard.

"You want to come, Dandelion?" I ask, drawing her panties down far enough that I can watch her fingers work over her sweet little pussy. I set my hands behind my head like I'm watching a fucking movie. "You want me to watch?"

She doesn't answer, doesn't have to. It takes all I have to hold back, but I do give myself a minute to take in how her fingers work over her slippery sex, and moan when she presses her wet pussy to my cock, using me to get herself off.

"Fuck," I groan and draw her panties up. Little good it does with her fingers still inside there. I can smell her arousal, and I want nothing more than to flip her onto her back and drive into her hard. Make her forget everything but me. But when she leans forward and brings her mouth to mine, I turn away, take her by the hips, and press her to me one more time before making myself move her off me.

"Come on," she protests, swinging one leg back over me. "You want me."

"No one's denying that." I flip her onto her back and hold her down, leaning my torso over her. "But I said no. If you want to get off, have at it. But I told you I'm not touching you now."

She exhales, annoyed, shoves me off, and turns her back to me. "Fine."

"Are you pouting?"

"Fuck off."

"I tell you what," I start, spooning her and wrapping an arm over her stomach. "I'll make you come twice when I do fuck you. What do you say to that?"

"I say fuck off."

I let her go. "Suit yourself." She pulls the blanket up over herself. "But I do have one question."

"What?" she snaps.

"Don't you want to wash your dirty little fingers?"

She flips me off with one of those fingers, and I chuckle before laying my arm across her again and tugging her close, this time not letting her go when she tries to wriggle free. I'm thinking instead not about being fucked up for wanting to sleep with the enemy but just about being fucked in general because what my brother and I set out to do has gone sideways. It's shifted so completely that as I listen to her breathe softly beside me, all I can think is I can't imagine going back to a life before her. A life without her.

## 14

## AMADEO

Bruno and I head to Tilbury's office after Bastian falls asleep. The clinic is attached to his house, which lies on several acres of land about an hour and a half outside the city. Knowing the sensitivity of his specialty, he's apparently used to meeting with clients at odd hours. And given the fact that just an initial appointment with the good doctor costs several thousand dollars, which he'll happily apply to your treatment, he's motivated. Although I know Bastian wanted to be here, it would have set off red flags for the doctor to see him in his state, so it's Bruno and me.

"The clinic itself houses up to six patients at a time," says the doctor's secretary. "The high walls ensure privacy, and they also keep our patients safe." Locked in is more like it given the security at the front gates.

She points out the patients' quarters, which Dr.

Tilbury will take us through later, apparently—so much for privacy—and we're buzzed in through another set of doors that lead to a space set up more like a house than a clinic.

"If you'll wait here, I'll let Dr. Tilbury know you've arrived."

Bruno and I look at each other, but before we even have a chance to sit down, the door she disappeared through opens, and a man in his late fifties stands before us in a thousand-dollar suit, his jet-black hair with a patch of well-positioned gray coiffed to perfection, not a single line on his face. I glance at Bruno and wonder if he's thinking the same thing. This man must keep his plastic surgeon on retainer.

"Gentlemen, I'm Dr. Tilbury. It's so good to meet you in person." He walks toward us, arm extended, and I think he'd have a compassionate, concerned look on his face if Botox allowed it. I don't like this man. Not one bit.

"Dr. Tilbury, I'm Bruno, and this is Amadeo. It's good to meet you."

"Oh, but I thought the brothers would come. You're their uncle? Is that right?"

"That's right," Bruno lies.

"My brother was under the weather, so Bruno accompanied me to the States. We didn't want to put off this meeting any longer. Mr. Russo was so positive about the work you did with his daughter, well, it's just what my sister needs."

He smiles. "Yes, you mentioned Mr. Russo in one of

our conversations. My condolences. He was a good man."

No comment.

"And Vittoria. Sweet child. Too young to carry such a burden," he says with a look as if he's reminiscing. It turns my stomach, and I really don't like how he refers to her as sweet. It has a creepy quality to it. "You know, Mr. Russo was one of the first to believe in my work," he says with a smile. Anything close to emotion has been erased from his eyes, an egotistical gleam replacing it. God complex.

"Was he?"

"Come into my office and we can talk. Tea, coffee? Something stronger?"

"No, thanks," I answer for us both as we're shown into Tilbury's oversized, luxurious office where he takes a seat behind his desk, and we're directed to sit on the leather chairs across from it. Behind him on the wall are various degrees. Apart from that, there is nothing personal. No photos of anyone, not even a dog. As far as I know, he's never married and never had children, nor does he have siblings.

He opens the laptop on his desk and puts a pair of reading glasses on. "Now about Hannah. She's fourteen, if I recall."

I grip the arms of the seat at the mention of Hannah's name, her age. So far, it's all the truth. But things are going to get trickier when he digs deeper. Good news is we have enough on him that he'll go along with what we need him to go along with.

"That was Vittoria's age, and you worked with her for about a year, is that right, Doctor?" I ask.

He types something, then turns back to us and removes his glasses. "That's right. Vittoria's case was complicated, and well, I was not as experienced as I am now. Your sister's case is less involved from what I gather. You can expect her to spend about four months, perhaps five, at the clinic. My methods have developed over time, their effectiveness and... thoroughness, depending on the patient's receptibility, of course." He leans toward us. "I'm sure I'm not failing to protect anyone's rights to privacy when I say Vittoria was of a difficult nature."

"How do you mean?"

"She was not so malleable. Easy to bend."

Did he really just say that of a fourteen-year-old girl in his care? The look in my eyes must alarm him because he clears his throat.

"Go on, Doctor," Bruno says. "We'd hold anything you say about any former patient in strictest confidence. Our visit here is a secret. And given the delicate nature of things, well, I think I can say we can all speak openly. We are, of course, prepared to pay substantially for any help you are able to provide."

Tilbury clears his throat. "Let's speak freely indeed." Because money talks. Fucking greedy bastard.

Bruno and I remain silent.

"I took custody of Vittoria within a few days of... the incident. She was a minor, and of course, given the circumstances, she wouldn't have been prosecuted and her name never released to the public, but these things have a way of getting out, don't they? Especially for a family such as theirs. Her father wanted to erase the event altogether. He wanted her unblemished. Pure. Like she had been. And I understand. He loved his daughter, and I believe it broke a piece of him to see her so broken." He stops to drink a sip of steaming lemon water from his glass on the desk. "But when I was finished, I'm happy to say I was able to give him his little girl back almost exactly as she was before."

"*Almost* exactly?" Bruno asks.

"Well, like I told you, I was not as experienced, and Vittoria's case was… shall we say extreme? Hannah will be delivered exactly as you want her."

I like these Stepford Wives vibes less and less.

"How was Vittoria's case extreme?" I ask, focusing on what I need to get out of this meeting.

He hesitates.

"Geno Russo is dead, Dr. Tilbury," I say, leaning my elbows on his desk. "I have no intention of sharing anything I learn here about Vittoria. I just want to be sure this is the right place and the best treatment for my sister."

He nods. "I was unable to isolate the event in Vittoria's case."

We wait.

"In the end, more time was erased than ideal, but it was erased. Now as to my methods," he says, changing the subject. I put a pin in it and watch as he directs our attention to the side wall, where a screen silently descends from the ceiling. "I use a specific type of hypnosis coupled with electroconvulsive therapy, ECT as you may know it..." he continues, but I stop listening because the room darkens, and an image fills the screen.

Vittoria.

My heart misses a beat as I take her in. She looks a lot like she does now just younger. So much younger. Her face is softer, more rounded, hair cut like a kid took scissors to it, and it looks like it hasn't been brushed in days. She's barefoot, wearing a hospital gown that is too big on her and she's alone in a padded room with a cot in one corner. Everything is pristine white and too bright. And Vittoria is pacing, pacing, pacing and muttering to herself. Every few minutes, she stops to look at her hands back and front, back and front, like I've seen her do a few times. But I see how red the skin of her hands is, and the blotches look raw. Her lips move, and although there's audio, we can't make out the words.

Dr. Tilbury, looking much like he does now, enters with two men in scrubs, and it's like a fucking horror movie. Vittoria stops dead, looks at him, then at them. She takes a step back and shakes her head. But then her expression changes. It softens. And I see Geno Russo come into the screen behind the doctor.

"Daddy." She tilts her head, then looks at her hands again, back and front before scratching her head almost violently. When she looks back up, her eyes are wet with tears. Against the doctor's orders, Geno Russo hugs his daughter, and I see him squeeze his eyes shut.

This is the same man who ordered his men to slice our faces, to smash my father's knees. The same man to whom a human life, a child's life, was worth fifteen hundred dollars. I can't reconcile the two.

"Daddy. I can't get them clean. I can't," Vittoria says, drawing back. "Tell them I need the bleach. Tell them I need it. I need it, or it won't come off. Daddy, tell them…"

"That's enough," I say, turning back to the doctor. He's watching as if entertained, as if all that's missing is a fucking tub of popcorn. I'm going to fucking kill him.

"But my methods—"

"Shut it off!"

He pauses, surprised. Vittoria's face freezes on the screen, and I can't look at it.

"What happened to her?" I ask in a voice I don't recognize.

"That's personal—"

Before I can think, I'm on my feet slamming both hands on his desk. "What the fuck happened to her?"

The doctor leans backward, and I see him reach for what I imagine is a button alerting security under his desk.

"Amadeo," Bruno says with a hand on my shoulder. He's up on his feet too. He shifts his attention to the doctor. "You can imagine how upsetting this is to Amadeo, considering his sister is the same age." He turns to me and gives me a look that says I'm about to fuck this up. "Sit."

Fine. But instead of sitting, I pace, and in the corner of my eye, I see the young Vittoria with her hair shorn, and the skin of her hands cracked and blotchy and raw and in her eyes a look I don't have words for.

"Perhaps this treatment isn't for Hannah," Dr. Tilbury says in a lowered voice to Bruno.

"We'll decide that. Can you be more specific about Ms. Russo's case, Doctor? How is it similar to my niece and how is it dissimilar?"

Tilbury nods, switches off the screen altogether, thank fuck, and sets his hands on his desk as the lights come back up. I sit on the edge of the couch set farthest away from the desk, lean my elbows on my knees, and lock my fingers together to keep from killing him before he gives us what we need.

"Vittoria Russo was attacked. Kidnapped, held prisoner, and raped by two men over a period of six days."

"Jesus," Bruno says.

I just stare at the man whose lips are moving but whose face is frozen as my brain tries to work out what I'm hearing.

"They kept her in a basement in one of Russo's properties. Abandoned still. I don't think he had the stomach to develop it after what happened. But that's not all. That's not why she keeps looking at her hands."

The image of her snatching Bastian's gun and shooting that man comes to mind. The look on her face. The determination with which she did it. The lack of hesitation. Lack of any emotion. And I understand.

"She killed them, didn't she?" I ask.

Tilbury looks at me for a long minute before he nods.

"How?"

"Got ahold of one of their guns. Her father found her soon after. Mere hours later. She began scrubbing her hands with bleach for days afterward. It's why we had her in there, nails clipped short so she wouldn't rip off skin. She'd use anything she could to scrub at her hands to get the blood off that only she could see."

"Which property?" I ask.

He looks confused. "I'm not certain, but it's in the city. I don't know why he didn't sell it. Get rid of it."

"The memories, can they return?"

"They're erased."

"Are you certain?"

"Well, of course the human mind is complex, isn't it?"

"Is that how you cover your ass?"

He ignores my comment. "There can be unforeseen triggers."

"Like?"

"Like a similar event happening to her or someone she knows. A news story. Stress. It can be any number of things. Like I said, the mind is complex," he reiterates.

"Do you have more video footage?" Bruno asks.

Tilbury hesitates, then looks at Bruno. "I record all my sessions. So I can learn from them of course."

"I'm sure. Who has seen these?" I ask.

He looks at me, then at Bruno.

"Who have you shown these to?"

"A few prospective clients like you."

"You fucking advertised using a fourteen-year-old girl's trauma?"

"I... it wasn't..."

I stalk across the room and swipe my arm across the desk, knocking his laptop and everything else to the floor. "You fucking used a fourteen-year-old girl's trauma to fucking promote yourself?"

He succeeds in pushing that button to call security as I lean over to grab him by the collar and drag him to his feet then over the desk. I get one good hit on his over-Botoxed face before two hulking men drag me off.

"I want all the recordings of Vittoria Russo," I tell him as I try to free myself from them while they hold tight, searching me and taking my pistol before dragging me toward the door.

"I'm sorry, I'm afraid that's out of the question," Tilbury says, straightening and adjusting his hair, which has shifted unnaturally.

"Get the fuck off me before I fucking kill you," I tell the guards. I imagine what they'd have done to someone Vittoria's size, and it makes me so fucking angry I can barely think.

Bruno stands, cool and collected as always as I throw the two behemoths off. "Dr. Tilbury," he starts, opening his briefcase. He retrieves a folder, then closes the case. "We will need those files," he says as he starts to lay out photos of the good doctor with the first of his young patients.

Tilbury swallows as Bruno sets another photo next to the first.

"Get out!" Tilbury yells to his goons. "Get out! Now!" They look confused, and I grab my gun.

"Get the fuck out," I tell them, and they take a look at what's on the desk and file out.

Bruno sets another photo down.

"Did you touch Vittoria?" I ask as I stalk toward him. He scurries behind his desk as if that will save him.

He shakes his head as I come around, take him by the collar, and slam him against the wall. "Did you fucking touch Vittoria Russo?"

"No! Not the girls. I... Not the girls."

"Yeah, well, you're going to stop touching the boys too."

"The recordings of Vittoria Russo. Where are they stored?" Bruno asks before I get ahead of myself. I don't know how he can keep such a level head when dealing with slime like this.

"Main server."

"Where is that?" I ask.

He points at a door, and I shove him toward it. He opens it, and there is a bigger than expected main server.

"Erase them."

"Even if I erased mine, her father would have had copies."

Fuck. "Anyone else?"

He shakes his head.

"Good. Erase them. In fact, erase all the sessions you recorded."

"I need them for my practice."

I slam his head into the wall to knock some sense into him, then right him and make him look at me. "Erase the fucking files or I'll erase you."

He nods frantically and glances at Bruno, who is still meticulously laying out photo after damning photo. I'm not sure how he obtained those, but that's why he gets paid what he gets paid. Tilbury pushes some buttons on the server, and I watch as file after file is deleted. When it's finished, I aim my gun at the box and empty the magazine into it. Tilbury screams as if I were shooting him.

The door opens, and the two men who just left rush back in. Bruno picks up his briefcase, and we walk toward the door.

"Excuse us," I say, pistol in my hand at my side. It's empty, but they don't know that.

"Those photographs have just been delivered electronically to the authorities. You may want to make yourselves scarce, gentlemen," Bruno says.

They look at each other, glance at the photos, and turn to rush out. I don't look back as Bruno and I walk out of that building and drive off the grounds, feeling like I need to bleach my fucking skin after that encounter.

Bleach.

Fuck.

Vittoria.

This explains things. It explains everything.

## 15

## VITTORIA

I wake up alone feeling groggy and even more exhausted after a restless night. I'm confused as I look around the unfamiliar surroundings. Light filters in from around the edges of the heavy drapes, and I roll onto my back to look up at the ceiling, then at the empty space beside me. I touch a hand to the pillow.

Remembering last night makes me flush hot with embarrassment. He rejected me. But I'm not sure what I was thinking by practically mounting him. I'd had the nightmare again and given the events of the day, I don't know. It messed with me even more than usual, and I didn't want to be alone.

I get out of bed quickly—too quickly because a dizzy spell hits, and I have to hold the nightstand as the room momentarily tilts, then rights itself.

A shower. I need a shower. Stripping off my bra and panties and trying not to think about last night, I step into the large, glass-walled stall and let water spray my face. Spray some sense into me. I need to figure out where my head is. I'm confused and upset. I'm glad that Bastian wasn't hurt worse than he is, but the fact that Lucien could command that kind of manpower and pull off what is essentially kidnapping and torture scares the hell out of me. What else is he capable of? And the comment about Dad not being surprised at the news of the accident. Was he just trying to fuck with me because I'm not sure Bastian thinks so.

But I need to keep a clear head right now. Today, I'll sign the necessary paperwork to transfer controlling shares of Russo Properties & Holdings to me. Well, to Amadeo, I guess. But I don't care. It doesn't matter. It can't. Even though there's a nudge of guilt over it. Over me handing over my father's dream to a man who hates him. Who will erase him. But once it's done, I can go back to Italy. Go to Emma. Maybe we'll even stay there. Live Dad's other dream.

Bruno said he had contacts who would push my application for guardianship of Emma through. That same contact would then handle Lucien's application. But that doesn't matter to me. He's not getting near Emma. I won't allow it. She's out of the country, and I'll keep her hidden as long as I have to in order to keep her safe from him.

I try to focus on the fact that by the end of the day, I'll be on my way back to Emma and this whole big mess will be mostly behind me. I should be happy. Well, as happy as someone in my situation can be, given all that's happened. But the thought of walking away, leaving Amadeo and Bastian, upsets me, and I don't know why. It makes no sense, but it does.

Once I'm finished showering, I grab a towel and wrap it around myself. I pick up my panties and bra from the floor and go back into the bedroom. My suitcase is in the room just two doors down, and I have my hand on the doorknob when I remember something. I turn back to Bastian's side of the bed and walk over to the nightstand. Those pills are still there, but the glass of water is empty.

I pull open the drawer where he'd crumpled and dropped the note that had been left for him, and I see it. Just a little wad of paper. I reach in to pick it up, my heart racing. Something tells me not to do it, to leave it alone and let it be.

But I'm not the leave it alone type. Never have been. So I flatten out the little scrap of paper and read it.

*Bruno and I are going to see Tilbury. Get some rest. I'll let you know what we find.*

The room goes sideways again, but this time, it isn't because I stood up too fast. I drop down onto the unmade bed and stare at the carpet, unseeing.

Tilbury. Dr. Tilbury.

I shiver with cold as the bedroom I'm in fades, and I'm in a windowless white room with white lights in the ceiling. They never turn those off, and it's too bright. I can't tell if it's night or day. The room smells like a hospital. I sit up, groggy, set my bare feet on the cold tiled floor and look at my hands. The skin is dry and cracked and red in places. My nails are cut so short they clipped skin.

I turn them over back and front and remember the feel of a gun in my hand. The weight of it. The antiseptic smell is gone then, replaced by an animal scent and blood and rot. I see the kneeling man in front of me in that barn and try to remember what I felt when I pulled the trigger. Try to remember what I thought.

Men's voices come closer, a door opening.

"Dandelion."

I blink, turn my hands over again. They're just my hands with the wedding band on one finger. The ring finger of my other hand empty.

"Dandelion."

I look up. Amadeo and Bastian stand in the doorway watching me. Bastian is fresh from a shower. Amadeo's suit is rumpled, and his usual five-o'clock shadow is denser. He looks older today. I study them both, seeing the similarities, the differences. Seeing how they're both looking at me with something different than usual.

But then their eyes move to the piece of paper in my hand, and mine do too, and I read it again. See that name again. I squeeze my eyes shut. Today is my birthday. I'm twenty-one years old. Not fourteen. I'm in Dominic Benedetti's penthouse. Not locked in a too-bright, too-antiseptic white room. I'm safe.

I open my eyes and see the skin of my hands again. Pull the towel off my head and let my wet hair drip down my back. It's long. Not shorn. I see a flash of the woman who cut it. Remember her meaty hands. Her meanness.

"Vittoria." It's Amadeo. He's standing just a few feet from me.

I stand up, show him the note in my hand although they've already seen it and know that I know.

"Is that where you went?" I crumple the scrap and chuck it at his chest.

It bounces off him and drops to the floor. He searches my face, takes my hands in his and looks down at them so I am looking at the top of his head, the thick dark hair. Bastian closes the door. I hear the click but don't look away as Amadeo turns my hands back and forth as if he's searching for something.

Afraid of what he'll find, I snatch my hands away and shove him backward. "Is that where you went?" I ask again, my lip curling around the words.

He nods gently, and it only pisses me off more.

"You put me to bed, then snuck out to go see what you could find on me?"

"It's not like that, Vittoria."

"Don't fucking call me that. I'm Dandelion to you. To you both! Let's stay on our sides of the boxing ring."

"We're not in a boxing ring," he says. Taking my hands again, he kisses the back of each one, then turns them over and kisses my palms, the tip of each finger.

My stomach flutters, and all I can do is watch because his touch is confusing. His gentleness is confusing.

I glimpse Bastian leaning against the wall. He's got his arms folded and is watching intently, and when I look at Amadeo again, he's looking at me.

"What did you learn, then? What did he tell you about me?" Because these two know something I don't. And I don't like the way they're watching me. Like they think I'm going to break or something.

"He filled in some gaps," Amadeo says, eyes intent on mine.

"So much for doctor-patient confidentiality," I say flippantly and try to take my hands from his, but he doesn't let me go. "What gaps?" I ask, hating that I'm at a loss. That I don't know what he could have told them. All I know is I'm afraid of it. Of them finding out whatever it is.

"Nothing that makes any difference. Nothing you need to worry about." He lets me go and checks his watch. "I need to have a shower." He turns toward the bathroom, but I catch his arm.

"What gaps?" I ask, stepping in front of him.

He looks me over, and that look, it's pity. It's fucking pity.

"Why the fuck are you looking at me like that?" I shove him again. They're both so big that I don't know why I bother. I can't usually budge them. "What did he say to make you look at me like that?"

Amadeo takes my wrists, his eyes growing darker. "What could he say?"

I'm confused. I blink away, glancing at Bastian. I

flush, remembering last night. But I turn my attention back to Amadeo.

"You had no right. You're invading my privacy."

At that, he chuckles, then walks me backward until my back hits the wall. "Your privacy, Vittoria? I think we're past that, don't you?" He shifts my wrists to one hand, and with a tug, the towel loosens and drops to the floor. He glances down, then brings his mouth to mine and kisses me, and I'm taken aback. Because Amadeo doesn't like kissing me. It does something to him. And to me.

I make a sound—it's not a protest so much as surprise—and I close my eyes and feel him. Just feel him.

"I like you, Dandelion," he says before taking my mouth again and swallowing anything I would have said. When he draws back to look down at me, his eyes are almost black. "I heard my brother promised to make you come twice." He grins, and Bastian chuckles from his place at the wall.

My skin flushes with heat. "Are you making fun of me?" I wriggle to get my wrists free, but his grin only widens as he holds tight. "Are you fucking making fun of me?"

"Maybe a little," he says as he dips his head to kiss my neck, then drops to his knees and releases my hands as he lifts one of my legs over his shoulder. He brings his mouth to my sex, and whatever response I had is gone. Poof. Vanished. All I can do is weave my fingers into his hair and moan as I drop my head back and bite my lip when I feel his wet tongue on me, inside me.

I open my eyes and meet Bastian's gaze across the room. His arms are still folded, and his eyes are locked on mine, and when Amadeo closes his mouth over my clit, it takes my breath away. I look down as I come, look at my hands in his hair. At the wedding band on one finger and the empty space on the other. And Bastian standing alone across the room. And I know at least one thing. One thing about the brothers. About my feelings for them. And that knowledge terrifies me.

## 16

## BASTIAN

I watch her come. Fuck. I can watch her come twenty-four-seven.

Amadeo rises to his feet, lifts a wilted Dandelion off hers, and carries her to the bed.

"Brother," he says, voice hoarse. "How do you want her?"

"On her hands and knees so I can see my options."

Amadeo turns to her. "You heard him."

She looks from Amadeo to me then back and gets on her hands and knees like a good girl. She lowers herself to her elbows and looks back at me, offering herself to me.

I grin and draw my shirt over my head as I take in the glistening lips of her pussy. So fucking inviting. I position myself behind and undo my jeans as my thumb glides over her pussy, her ass.

"You have a preference, Amadeo?" I ask as I spread her arousal back and forth.

"I'm happy with either," Amadeo says.

I grin, grip her hips, tug her closer, and make my choice. I thrust into her pussy hard, making her grunt as her walls squeeze my dick before stretching around it.

"You like that, Dandelion?" I ask, taking a fistful of hair and hauling her torso up.

She nods.

"Good. Now I want you to do something for me." She nods again, moaning. "I want you to put your dirty little fingers on your clit and play with yourself. A little show as Amadeo waits his turn while I fuck your tight cunt."

She does as she's told, and I hold her to me as I take her. Amadeo tugs his shirt off popping some buttons in his haste as he moves across the room to watch her play with herself, her moans and gasps melting into one as I thrust, holding tight to her. She comes before I've really gotten started. She's a ball of nerves already, alternately begging for more and begging me to stop. I let her drop to her hands and shift my focus to watch my cock disappear inside her, and when I'm ready to come, I hook a finger into her other hole and watch her collapse on the bed, panting as she comes again, squeezing my dick and my finger as I release inside her.

I draw out, come spilling down her thighs, and step away. Amadeo takes his place behind her, and she protests, but I take her face in my hands and kiss her. Her hands cover mine.

"Are you ready for me, Dandelion?" He adjusts her position so her hips are tilted at the right angle. I know the moment he pushes into her ass when she whimpers into my mouth, her fingernails digging into my wrists as she stretches to take the thickest part of him.

"Relax. Open for him."

"I... can't take more."

"You can. You will. Look at me."

She holds tight to me, eyes huge, and I watch her expression change as pain turns to pleasure. Amadeo finds his rhythm, stretching her slowly, then, once she's ready, taking her hard as she cries out, orgasm overtaking her as she holds tight to me with one hand, the other stretched back to take Amadeo's.

When it's finished and he pulls out, we clean her and lie together on the bed, the three of us with our Dandelion in the middle. She kisses my mouth, then turns to Amadeo and kisses his. He holds her gaze, and I think about the things Amadeo told me about his visit to Tilbury. What they did to her. What she did.

"What did he tell you about me?" she asks in a near whisper as if reading my mind.

"Nothing that matters, Dandelion. Close your eyes. No one's ever going to hurt you again. You're safe now."

She blinks, and I think she's going to ask a question, but something gives inside her. I can almost see it. She nods, closes her eyes. Maybe it's easier this way. I hope so because I don't ever want her to remember what happened to her. And I'm grateful when her face and body relax, and she drifts off to sleep.

We leave Vittoria to sleep while we make our plans.

"Lucien Russo has vanished into thin air," Amadeo says.

"Expected as much. He'll reappear once we're gone."

Amadeo nods. "Dominic's men will keep an eye on that. But that's not priority right now."

"Dandelion."

He nods. "I want her out of this city. Out of his reach."

She's due at Brady's office at the end of the afternoon to sign the paperwork that will transfer her inheritance.

Amadeo told me about what he'd learned. Described the video he'd seen, and I can imagine the ones he didn't. We're now scrolling through page after page of Russo's undeveloped properties to find the one where those men had taken her. I swear Russo owned half the East Coast.

"He'd have had her guarded," Amadeo says. "No way two men could just get to her."

We need to find out their names, but we've been through death notices and police incidents for a month around the time she was admitted as an inpatient of Tilbury, but nothing matches what we need. Although it's not surprising. I'm thinking Russo had the bodies disposed of and everything neatly covered up.

"She always seemed a little off, but do you think it's been worse since what happened in Naples?"

"Yeah, I do. And it makes sense. Let's get the paperwork signed today and get her back to Italy. She'll stay at the Ravello house. I want to find out what happened exactly. Find the property and see who had access."

"Who had access to what?"

We both turn to find Vittoria standing in the entryway of the dining room. It's an open floor plan so no doors.

"You have to stop creeping up on people, Dandelion," I tell her. She's showered, wet hair braided on either side of her face. She's wearing jeans and a close-fitting T-shirt with a pair of Chucks. No makeup on her face. She is stunning.

"I'm not creeping," she says. "You two were so involved in whatever you're looking at you didn't hear me."

She walks toward us, and Amadeo closes the laptop as we both stand. She looks at it, then at us. "Who had access to what?"

Amadeo looks her over and nods. "You look well rested."

"Well fucked you mean."

"Well fucked," he says, smiling.

I watch the two of them. I'm not jealous, per se. I was, but it's gone. But they have something I don't. Those rings on their fingers.

When I shift my gaze to Vittoria, I see she's watching me. I'm not sure if she's conscious of the motion as she turns her wedding band around while holding my gaze.

"Once I sign the papers, I'll fly home?"

"Home?" I ask, surprised.

She shakes her head like it was just a mistake. "To Italy. To get Emma."

"To get her?" Amadeo asks.

She shifts her gaze to him. Her smile vanishes. "You said after I signed, you'd let us go."

*He said what?* I look to my brother, curious about his answer.

Amadeo sighs. "I want to be sure you're both safe, Vittoria."

She shakes her head. "No. We had an agreement. You said you'd set us free after you get what you want."

*He said what?*

"The shares, control of the company, all of my money, it's yours. I have nothing else to give you."

"When it's time, I will set you free. You have my word."

She snorts. "Your word means less and less. I'm going to get Emma, and we're leaving. That's the end of that." She turns to walk away, but Amadeo goes after her, catching her arm, and spins her around.

"You'll go when it's safe. Not before."

She tries to tug free, but he doesn't let her go. "And who will decide when it's safe? Let me guess. You?"

"Vittoria—"

"No. Dandelion. Just call me Dandelion." She tries again to tug free.

"Vittoria."

"What?" she snaps.

He touches her face, tilting her chin up so she

looks at him, and I'm surprised at this gentle touch. This caring side of my brother that I rarely see. He's only this caring with our mother, if I think about it.

"What?" she asks, tone a little quieter. I wonder if she's affected by that tenderness.

But before he can answer, Bruno turns the corner, and the moment is gone.

"Time to go," he announces. "There are two cars with guards downstairs."

Vittoria takes the opportunity to break free.

"I'll ride with you," she tells him. "And then I'm leaving," she says to Amadeo.

We watch her walk away, Bruno with one eyebrow raised.

"Go ahead," Amadeo tells him, and we watch them walk out the door.

I turn to him when we're alone. "What did you agree with her, brother?"

His jaw tightens. "That I'd set her free once it was over."

We look at each other for a long, long minute. Thing is, there was a time I would have said hell no to that. I would have rather locked her away in a cell somewhere than let her go to live a life. To have a life at all.

Now, I still say hell no. But for a different reason.

"She's not going anywhere," I say.

"No. She's not."

I nod, glad we're in agreement. "Let's go get this over with."

## 17

## AMADEO

She neither speaks nor looks at my brother or me throughout the hour-and-a-half meeting with Brady as she signs where he tells her to sign and nods along as he explains things she isn't even listening to. She wants to be finished and leave. It may be best for her anyway. I need her out of New York City and out of reach of her brother, so I'll give her half of what she wants. She'll go to Italy to be with her sister. But she won't be leaving the Ravello property.

Once we're finished, Brady hands her a folder. "Details of what I told you are inside as well as specifics about your allowance," he says with a glance at me. He doesn't like that I have control of her finances. I get it. He knew her father and his loyalty will be with Vittoria. But this business he doesn't know about, and I don't much give a fuck what he thinks of it or me.

"My *allowance*," she says bitterly, sending a scathing

look my way, the first in all the time we've been in this office.

"Access codes and everything you need are in your folder. Read it, Vittoria. Understand the details and your rights."

"I'll have access to the money right away? My *allowance*."

"Right away." He gestures to the folder.

"Can he stop paying it?" she asks him.

"I won't," I answer before Brady can open his mouth.

I watch her jaw tighten, but she nods, then stuffs the envelope into a large tote she'd brought with her. I turn to Brady. "Work on all site stops today. You put the word out yet?"

"What?" Vittoria asks.

"Construction is paused until further notice," I tell her.

She studies me, but I turn to Brady and raise my eyebrows, waiting for his response.

"There are quite a few sites, Mr. Caballero. It will take time."

"But you've got it under control?"

"Yes, sir," he says, clearly not pleased. I could give a fuck.

"Good." I turn to Vittoria. "Bruno will take you to the airport," I take the keys to the penthouse and stand.

She recognizes the keys. "I want to go home first. To the penthouse."

"Why?"

"I want to get a few things for Emma and myself. And see it again. Maybe for the last time."

"That's dramatic," Bastian mutters from where he's leaning against the wall.

She doesn't acknowledge his comment. I look at Bruno. "Will that work?" We have a time slot at the airport. If we miss it, it will delay us for a few hours.

He checks his watch. "Should. We've got an hour."

"Okay."

Brady clears his throat. "A word, Mr. Caballero."

"Right now? We're a little pressed for time."

"It won't take long."

"Fine. We'll meet you at the penthouse," I tell Bruno, tossing him the keys. He nods and takes Vittoria out.

Once they're gone, Brady dismisses the assistant who is taking notes and waits until the door is closed to turn his gaze to me. He's an intelligent man. And from the way he's talked to Vittoria, I think he is concerned for her welfare. Still, there's something about him I don't like. But that's probably my untrusting nature. Most people can't be trusted. I know this.

I make a point of checking my watch.

"I want to tell you something that may be overstepping the parameters of my role, but given what I know and how things stand, I feel it is my duty to Ms. Russo." He shakes his head. "Mrs. Caballero."

"Go on, Mr. Brady," I say.

He walks to the window, and I'm not sure he's going to continue until he turns back around and returns to his desk.

"Mr. Russo loved that girl. She was a bright light in a sometimes dreary life."

"Perhaps it was dreary for the choices he made, Mr. Brady. I thought I was here to sign papers, but if you're going to waste my time singing that man's praises..." I start, standing. I'm not going to sit here and listen to him glorify Geno Russo as if he were some fucking saint.

"She's gone through hell. You should know that."

Now I'm curious. "Go on."

He shakes his head. "I can't divulge details, but I hope to appeal to your humanity."

"Now you insult me."

"This isn't a game. I don't like you. I don't like what you've managed to do."

"I don't care."

"Just don't hurt her. She doesn't deserve it." He says it with such an authentic tone, with such a look in his eyes that it catches me off guard, and I find I don't have a comeback.

"She'll be fine. It's not her I intend to punish."

"Good. Because if something were to happen to her, if she were hurt or worse, I would go to the authorities."

I grin. "How lucky the Russos are to have such a devoted lawyer working for them. Happen to know where Lucien Russo is?"

"No," he answers too quickly. Getting up, he walks to the printer set behind his desk and picks up the sheet lying there. He sets it on his desk and signs it, then hands it to me. "My resignation. I won't work with criminals."

I look at it and snort. "Who do you think you've been working with?"

"I've already named my temporary replacement until you find someone more suitable for your needs. I won't wish you luck, Mr. Caballero." With that, he buttons his jacket, and walks out of the office.

"Asshole," Bastian says.

Irritated, I toss the letter aside and take out my phone. I send a text to Dominic's man, the one in charge of the soldiers he's put at our disposal while we're here. He's in the lobby and responds immediately when I tell him to have someone follow Brady.

"What was that?" Bastian asks when I tuck the phone away.

"I put a tail on him. I don't trust him. Let's go. We have shit to do."

He nods. We head out to the elevators and out of the building to our SUV and drive together to the penthouse, which is only about a fifteen-minute ride. Lucien Russo lived here up until just a few days ago. The doorman, who has been alerted to our arrival, shows us to the elevator. Bastian and I ride to the top.

The building is beautiful, as I'd expect, and when the doors open onto the penthouse, I'm not surprised at its opulence. The large space boasts floor-to-ceiling windows with incredible views over the city. With an open floor plan, the kitchen, dining, and living rooms are one big open space and off three separate corridors are what I assume are bedrooms. Bruno is sitting on the extra-long chesterfield. He stands when we enter.

"Not bad, huh?" he asks as I take it in.

"Wouldn't expect anything less. Any word on Lucien's whereabouts?"

He shakes his head. "Nothing."

Bastian walks over from the kitchen biting into an apple. "Where's Vittoria?"

Bruno gestures down one of the corridors to the slightly open door. "She grabbed a few things mostly for the little girl. I checked the bag. It's just books and toys."

"Thanks."

"We'll need to leave in a few minutes."

Bastian and I walk toward the room Bruno pointed at and find Vittoria sitting behind the large desk studying a photo. When she shifts her eyes to us, they're sad.

"Are you okay?" I ask her.

She shrugs a shoulder and stands, tucking the photo, frame and all, into her tote. "Are you going to sell it?"

"Not yet. Anything missing?"

"You want an inventory? Are you afraid my brother stole something that belonged to us before he left?"

"Just asking, Dandelion. What did you put in your bag?"

She rolls her eyes, then reaches into her tote to show me a photo of herself and her father. It's fairly recent, and she's got her head on his shoulder as he snaps a selfie.

"Oh, also this." She takes out a second of her and her mother. She's young in this one. Maybe twelve. "Is that okay, or do you think I'll somehow turn them into weapons?"

"It's fine."

"Unless you want to search me, I'm ready to leave."

A dozen of Benedetti's men will accompany Bruno and her to the airport, and two of our own will be on the flight with them.

She turns to go, but Bastian, who is standing at the door, closes it. She turns back to me.

"I'm doing this for you, Vittoria. I want you safe."

She meets my eyes. "Are you stopping construction on all the sites to keep me safe too?"

"No. That has nothing to do with you."

"Of course it does. It's my legacy."

"Your father's legacy."

She shakes her head. "If I hadn't come to Italy, if I hadn't accompanied my father's body, how would you have done it?"

"Doesn't matter anymore, does it?"

"I just want to know how much of this is on me. Because me being there, you raiding the church and kidnapping me, then forcing me to marry you, it was all for this. Exactly this. I made it easy for you by showing up like that, didn't I?"

I sigh. "Don't think of it like that, Vittoria."

"Your talk of my safety is bullshit, Amadeo. I'm your prisoner. Let's call it what it is."

"You're hardly a prisoner."

"You may not lock me in a room for now, but I'm still your prisoner. Both of yours."

"For fuck's sake, are we back to this?" I'm growing impatient.

Bastian steps in, takes her, and turns her to face him. She looks up at him. He takes her hands, and I see his fingers move to the empty ring finger of her right one. I wonder if that's conscious.

I step back and watch. She doesn't pull away. She's angry with me, not him. Or at least she knows she needs an ally, and he seems to be her choice for that. Same as last time when we took her to the barn with us.

"You're not a prisoner. Not anymore. No one will lock you in any room. Understand?" he says.

She shrugs a shoulder and shifts her gaze away. He tilts her face up to his.

"Give us two days. We'll talk again once we're in Italy."

"Why do you need to stay? What are you going to do?"

"Need to look into a few things," I say. She turns to me, eyes narrowed. "Dandelion, don't look at me like that." She doesn't respond to me but to Bastian.

"Two days," she says.

"You're cute when you're angry," he says.

"Which is a good thing since you're angry a lot," I add, moving toward her and tugging on one of her braids.

With a sigh, she looks down, then finally up at me. "I trusted you. I know you can make me do whatever you want, but just remember that I trusted your word. Please don't let me have been wrong to do that."

In her eyes is such a raw emotion, an open wound, that I find myself unable to speak. She's right. I swallow over the lump in my throat and nod. A knock on the door interrupts us, and Bruno pokes his head in.

"We need to go, or we'll lose our time slot."

"Yeah, okay," I say, and Bastian and I both step away. She doesn't say another word or even look at either of us. Instead, she makes her way out of the room, leaving Bastian and me alone in the penthouse.

"She'll be all right," Bastian says.

"I know, and I'm sure this isn't easy for her."

"Let's take a look around. I'll find Lucien's office."

I nod and take the seat behind Geno Russo's desk.

---

BASTIAN AND I SPEND TWO HOURS IN THE PENTHOUSE. Geno's office was in pretty decent order, but if he kept anything of importance there, it's gone now. Lucien's office, on the other hand, looked like someone bulldozed it. Or, more accurately, shredded every single piece of paper in it and left the mess like confetti all over the floor.

The bedrooms are pretty generic like no one really lived here. I'm sitting on Vittoria's bed flipping through a book on the nightstand when Bastian walks in.

"Bruno texted. Flight took off without a hitch."

I close the book, set it aside, and stand. "Good."

"You got the password to the desktop?"

"Yeah. Brady passed it along. Why?"

Bastian holds up a thumb drive. "Found it taped to the bottom of a drawer in Lucien's bedroom."

That gets my attention. I follow Bastian to the study, switch the computer on and type in the password. Very tricky. It's Vittoria's birthday. Bastian plugs the thumb drive in. He sits behind the desk to open the single folder on the drive, and I stand behind him and watch as the first photo fills the screen.

It's startling what I see. At first, I think it's Vittoria. But he clicks to the second image, then the third.

"It's her mother," I say.

"Leah Russo." He clicks to the next one. They're obviously taken over a period of time because she's wearing different clothes in different seasons. She is as beautiful as Vittoria and so recognizable. In fact, she could be Vittoria's slightly older sister. Her hair is exactly like Vittoria's, a wild mane of blond waves that won't be tamed, and her eyes are as blue and as sad. They share many similar features with one very noticeable difference. The furrow between the older woman's eyebrows and the way she seems to be looking over her shoulder in so many of the shots.

But that changes as she enters a hotel lobby with her scarf pulled tight around her neck and her hat low on her forehead. Her hair is hidden in a single thick braid down her back, and she bypasses the lobby to disappear into the elevator. The photographer shot a series of images, catching her second after second as she searches the lobby before the doors close, her expression anxious.

The next set are taken on the same day but possibly by a different photographer stationed elsewhere because she's wearing the same clothes, hasn't even pulled her hat off or her scarf down as she enters a hotel room, her smile huge, eyes bright as she is embraced by a tall man with dark hair. It's obviously not Geno Russo from the build. This man has about thirty pounds on him. Where Geno was lean, this man is as tall but built differently, his arms thick with muscle and, we see in the next image when his shirt comes off, covered in ink.

Bastian clicks through the images of the couple undressing, then in bed.

"Wait. Go back."

He does, and I peer closer to see the purplish bruises around Leah Russo's neck and arms. Bastian sees it at the same time I do.

"You think he was beating her? Russo?"

Bastian zooms in as he shakes his head. "Don't know."

We get to another image taken in the lobby. Her cheeks are flushed with color, and her eyes contain a sheen that wasn't there in the previous shots. Leah Russo is clearly on her way out after a long afternoon spent in her lover's bed. But as the shadows fall over the city, so do they darken her eyes as she leaves the hotel and reenters her world, her life.

"She looks scared," I say.

"Probably afraid of getting caught."

I see the timestamp in the corner of this image.

"Look at that," I say, pointing at the bottom corner of the image.

"Not quite six years ago."

"Are you doing the math?"

"Already have."

"I want to see the man's face." But in all the photos, he's obscured in some way almost as if it were done on purpose. Did her lover set her up?

Bastian shakes his head as we click through more and more images. "Those tattoos, though, I'll send the file to Bruno. See what he can find."

"Good idea. So Lucien was having his stepmother followed. Do you think he shared those with Dad?"

Bastian shrugs a shoulder. "Why else take the photos? Unless he wanted to blackmail her, but what would he have to gain?"

"I wonder if he even needed to share them once Emma was born. He'd suspect even if he wouldn't know for certain after taking one look at Emma, I'm sure. He could have run DNA tests."

"Let's get those to Bruno and make sure Vittoria never sees them."

"Agreed." He removes the drive and drops it into his pocket.

"Ready to go?" I ask.

"Yeah." Neither of us is looking forward to the next part of our day.

We ride down on the elevator and climb into our SUV. Bastian settles himself behind the steering wheel as my phone dings with a message. It's Bruno.

"Bruno's got something."

Bastian glances at me but focuses on traffic.

"According to the financial reports Brady sent, there's one name that stands out, Anders Construction. It's apparently a shell company Bruno recognized. It's owned by Dmitri Anders, a businessman with known ties to the Russian mafia who recently found himself in some trouble with the American authorities. The payments were made out of Russo Properties & Holdings and came at irregular intervals, but that made little sense. He's following up with Brady and gathering more information on Anders."

"Russian mob? No shit."

"It would explain the soldiers who grabbed you. Based on what I heard, at least some were Russian."

"I'd like to know where he is, fucking spineless bastard."

"He'll turn up." I enter the directions to the first empty Russo property within a twenty-mile radius of the penthouse. There are three.

We sit in silence for a while. I know what's coming. What's on my brother's mind.

"You shouldn't have told her you'd let her go," Bastian finally says as we merge into traffic.

"Moot point. We're not."

"We decide these things together, brother."

I nod because he's right. I study his profile as he drives, remembering how she was with him. How he held her hand, traced the empty ring finger of her right hand.

"The reasons we're keeping her, Bastian," I start. Bastian glances my way, then focuses on the road. "They've changed for me."

"I'm not blind."

"I think they've changed for you, too."

His jaw tenses, but he nods once.

"Are we on the same page, then?" I ask.

"You mean are we keeping her because we want her for ourselves?"

I nod. It's confronting when it's so blatantly spelled out.

"Yeah, brother, same page, same sentence, same word."

"Not sure where Dandelion's head is but, well, one step at a time."

Silence again fills the space and for the next ten minutes we are each lost in our own thoughts.

"First property is coming up here on the right." The energy in the SUV shifts as we near the fenced off property with the big Russo Properties & Holdings sign in front.

Bastian pulls up in front. "This isn't the one," he says as he kills the engine, and we climb out.

"Too busy. Too public." The neighborhood is bustling. I use the key Brady gave me to unlock the gate. We need to be sure. We walk through the fencing, then onto the site, which consists of a trailer containing a desk, a drip coffee machine with a burnt pot on it, and an ashtray with cigarette butts still inside. And dust about an inch thick. What was here has been torn down, so if there was a basement, it's gone now.

"Let's go," Bastian says. "We're wasting our time here."

The second property is similar to the first although a little farther out of town. It has more privacy, and the structure hasn't been demolished yet, but the basement is more of a crawl space, so we head to the third. This one is the farthest way but still not too far. It's also the most private with a large, fenced-off lot. Just behind the fence is a run-down row of houses that reminds me of old horror movies.

We're quiet as we walk toward the open door of the center house. There's no trailer here. No office setup. The property had been bought eight years ago but never got as far as that. The lot itself is overgrown with weeds, and all that can be heard from the nearest neighborhood are muffled car horns and the occasional shout of someone. In other words, no one will be walking past this site unless they have reason to be here.

I glance at my brother as we enter. We split up—I go right, he goes left—and walk through the first floor. We don't need to go upstairs. There are three basements, one for each of the houses. I use my phone to light the way down to one, but it's small and crammed with old furniture that I can't imagine anybody would have space to move in there.

Bastian and I meet in the middle. He shakes his head and our gazes fall on the entrance of the basement of this last house. The door here is intact, and although the deadbolt has been broken, it is about the only thing that hasn't rusted in the place.

Without a word, I switch on the flashlight of my phone and shine it down the stairs.

"This is it," Bastian says. "I feel it."

I know what he's feeling. A dark thing. I think you could keep bars of gold unlocked down here and they'd be safe. My skin is crawling, and if I didn't have to go down there, I wouldn't.

Bastian switches on his flashlight and follows me down the rickety stairs.

"Careful," I tell him about a step that's broken. We get down to the concrete floor and I shine my light over the bare walls, the boxing bag hanging from a beam at the far end, the small outdoor table that's rusted, the empty beer bottles on top and broken glass on the floor. I walk to the cooler and find more bottles of beer inside, these unopened. I check the date on one. It's long expired. I assume there was ice in there once, but that water has long since evaporated.

But apart from that, I don't see more.

A large flashlight sits on the floor by the chair. I pick it up and switch it on. It blinks, then, to my surprise, goes on. I shine the brighter light over what I've found, but there's nothing more.

"Brother," comes Bastian's voice from behind the boxing bag. I know from his tone that he's found something. I walk over and duck my head to follow him into this second room. It's as large as the first but even more isolated. No small windows, no nothing. Just black. But I turn the flashlight onto the room, and my blood turns to ice.

"Fuck."

Along the far wall is a grimy mattress on a cot with a missing leg leaning half on the filthy floor. Chains hang from the ceiling, the cuffs empty now. A bucket lies on its side by the cot, and another table, chair, and more cans of beer are in here, too. In the farthest corner is a cage like you'd use for a big dog. Inside it is a dog dish. And attached to one of the bars of the cage is a set of handcuffs. On the wall over the cage is an old clock with a bullet hole through the center of it.

"They kept her here for six days," I say, remembering the image of Vittoria on that screen, the look in her eyes, the senseless muttering, her asking for bleach to clean her hands. To clean the blood of the bastards who hurt her off her hands.

"Blood," Bastian says. He's got the light from his

phone's flashlight on a spot on the mattress. I go to him and see it, that deep almost black of old blood. I shine the light over the walls and see what looks like spray paint there, but it's blood, too. "Why wouldn't he burn this place to the ground?"

I shake my head. "No fucking clue. Let's go. There's nothing more down here."

When we get back out into the light of the afternoon sun, we both stop to take a deep breath in. But that stench of basement clings to my nostrils.

"His properties are locked up tight. From the fencing to whatever is within," I say.

"Only one person would have access," Bastian adds as he walks into the overgrown grass and looks around. I know what he's looking for. A grave.

We're talking about the same person. The only person who would have cause to hurt Vittoria like that. To break her like only something like this would.

"I need a drink," I say.

"Me too."

## 18

## VITTORIA

They aren't going to let me go. I know this. And as confused as my own feelings are, I have to think of Emma.

Bruno seems busy with something and leaves me alone for the most part, so the flight to Ravello is quiet. Once we're in Naples, I'm ushered into a waiting SUV and driven straight to the Ravello house while Bruno returns to his home in the city.

Once I'm settled in the SUV, I take the envelope Mr. Brady gave me out of my purse and open it. I actually opened it on the flight, but when I saw what was inside, I discreetly tucked it back into my purse before Bruno or the soldiers could see. Now the two are riding in the front, and I'm alone in the back seat.

I take out the stack of papers. A lot of it is just copies of what I signed and what it means. I set most of those aside. I'll look those over later. One gives me details of the bank account where Amadeo will deposit my monthly allowance. I find a debit card, a credit card, and two wads of cash. The brand-new hundred-dollar bills are secured with a rubber band in an envelope inside the larger envelope. At a quick glance, there's maybe ten thousand dollars in here. But best of all, there's a cell phone. I leave it switched off and drop the whole lot into my purse. This gives me options I didn't have before.

I sit back in my seat and watch the blue sky and bluer ocean as we drive toward the Ravello house. When we arrive, my smile is genuine when the front door opens. Emma comes rushing out with Hyacinth behind her, and Nora and Francesca behind them. All of them are smiling and looking happy. Emma has rosy cheeks, and the shadows under her eyes are almost gone. She looks like a child of five should look.

"Emma!" I rush to her, set my tote on the ground, and hug her tight.

She pulls away but tugs at my hand as Hyacinth comes to give me a hug too. She tells Emma to give me a minute, but Emma shakes her head vehemently.

"We have a surprise for you," Nora says, unable to help herself as she takes Emma's other hand. Emma smiles up at her, and it's amazing what a difference these few days in this house have made for my quiet, frightened sister. I wonder if it's all the women around her and all the attention and love they're showering her with. The soldiers keep to the periphery for the most part.

"What surprise?" I ask Emma as I retrieve my tote

from the ground. Her smile grows huge as they lead me into the kitchen. The counters are dusted with flour, and the sink is full of bowls, but on the table is a beautiful birthday cake, homemade with pink icing and colorful sprinkles and a badly written Happy Birthday, Vitto on it.

I swipe icing with my finger and taste it as I giggle. "Who's Vitto?"

Emma shrugs her shoulders and puts her hands up smiling a naughty smile I'm so happy to see on her little face.

"We ran out of icing," Nora says with a laugh.

Emma goes to her, takes her hand, and leads her to the cabinet in the corner. She opens it and points at a shelf she can't reach.

"Ah, yes! Candles!"

"Sit down," Hyacinth says. "Time for cake."

I sit, setting my tote at my feet, unwilling to be parted from it because it's our way out. It's our only way.

---

That night, I lie in bed with Emma and wait for her to fall asleep. I doze as I do, tired from the travel. I wonder if Mr. Brady has gotten the word out to all the sites yet to stop construction. I can imagine how much it will cost, but this is their plan. It was all along. My coming to Italy to bury my father just made it easier for them to initiate things. Hell, my father dying was a stroke of luck for them.

Feeling nauseous at the thought, I sit up. Emma doesn't stir as I slip out of bed and leave her room, taking my tote bag with me. I haven't left it out of sight since getting here.

The house is dark, and when I get to the library, I see it's past midnight. I switch on a light, set the bag down, and am pouring myself a whiskey just as a soldier opens the library door, clearly alerted. I guess this is a good test of whether or not I'm a prisoner.

"What are you doing?" he asks.

"I'm going to read some riveting legal paperwork and drink some of this excellent whiskey." I raise my glass to him in a mock toast and drink. "Why don't you call your bosses and tell them?"

"No need," he says. "Don't go outside."

"Yes, sir." I salute him, then pretend he's not standing there as I carry my glass to the couch where I curl up, taking the folder out of my bag as he closes the door behind himself. Once he's gone, I set the legal papers aside and take out the phone. I switch it on, expecting it to be empty, but find one contact on it. My brother.

I remember our conversation. His response when I asked him about Hannah. As far as he was concerned, they were in love. The thought of a grown man having thought that, believed it, makes me shudder. But which is worse? Believing that or raping a girl? Is he truly possible of the latter? Is he fucked up enough to believe the former? I understand it was rape either way. She was too young to make that decision for herself, and he was already a grown man. But what was going on in Lucien's head?

Lucien and I have never been close. Not remotely so. He doesn't like me. Never has. He's made no secret of the fact. I understand it now. My mother was Dad's mistress while he was married to Lucien's mother. When she got pregnant, he set his wife aside and married Mom. I get why Lucien hates me. Why he blames me. Maybe I would be the same if I'd been in his shoes and he in mine.

Growing up, Dad always made sure he or someone he trusted was around when he was on business or traveling with Mom. When I was little and Lucien deigned to play with me, he decided the game and he made the rules. At first, I was happy to have someone to play with. I didn't have a lot of contact with other kids growing up, but the more I got to know Lucien, the less I wanted to be around him. Even as young as I was, I felt the danger of it.

More than a few times, I got hurt. The worst was a broken arm. Dad was furious, and I know he punished Lucien fiercely even though I tried to tell him it was an accident. He seemed to believe it wasn't. And I can't remember what I believed. What I knew, though, was that if Dad punished him today, Lucien would punish me tomorrow. I learned to steer clear of him for the most part. Soon after that, he was sent to boarding school, so I only saw him during holidays and summers.

But even given all of this, rape is something else. A different sort of violence. And with Hannah having been so young, I just can't wrap my brain around it. I don't want to believe it.

A banner alerting me to a text flashes across the screen. It looks like two messages were sent hours ago, but since I just turned the phone on and it picked up a signal, they're only now delivering. The messages are from Lucien. I read the first one.

Him: *Vittoria. I instructed Brady to put the phone and the cash in your envelope. He told me they didn't search you. Let me know when you're online.*

I pause for a moment, not expecting this. I read the second text.

Him: *Believe it or not, I am trying to help you. And yes, I'm doing it for myself as much as you. You've always thought me selfish, and you're right. I am. Call or text me. Hear me out.*

Me: *I'm here.*

Him: *I'm glad they didn't find the phone.*

Me: *What do you want?*

Him: *Those crooks you've got yourself mixed up with are no good. They will steal what is ours. What would be for the children you or I will have one day. And they will destroy Dad's legacy. I know you don't want that. They kidnapped you and Emma. They've stolen your inheritance. I will get you out of there and have that marriage annulled.*

*No judge will let it stand. Not to mention their enemies. They will come after you, too. You're a target.*

I consider his message and type my response.

Me: *Why do you care? You hate Emma and me. You've made that abundantly clear.*

Him: *Like I said, I'm selfish. I want what's mine.*

The thought that Amadeo and Bastian aren't going to let me go circles around my brain as I respond.

Me: *How can you help us?*

Lucien: *I have a contact in Naples. A powerful contact.*

Me: *??*

Lucien: *He can get you both out.*

Me: *Out to where? Are we just going to be someone else's prisoner?*

Lucien: *For fuck's sake, do you want my help or not?*

Me: *What I want is to be free.*

Lucien: *?*

Me: *Who is it? Your contact?*

Lucien: *Their uncle. He hates them.*

Uncle Sonny. I shake my head. Am I surprised he's Lucien's ally? What does it say about my brother? I glance up at Amadeo's desk and notice the leatherbound book they'd given me to read sitting on it. I guess someone brought it downstairs over the past few days. I think about what it accuses Lucien of. Think about the Lucien I know.

Lucien: *I can't believe this is something you need to think about. I didn't think you had a lot of options, sis.*

I hate when he calls me sis. It's said with a vehemence I can feel. Like he's spitting the word.

Me: *I need to go. I'll let you know tomorrow.*
Lucien: *Tomorrow may be too late.*
Me: *I need to go. Soldiers.*

It's a lie, but it doesn't matter. I switch off the phone and set it aside then stand to get the album from the desk. I open it to the article about Hannah, and I start to read.

## 19

## BASTIAN

Amadeo and I are having a drink before turning in for the night when his cell phone rings. He glances at the screen as I pour us another glass of Dominic Benedetti's excellent whiskey. We're still staying at his penthouse in the city while he's out of town with his wife and family.

"This is Amadeo," my brother says. I don't hear what the caller says, but Amadeo's expression changes. "Just a minute, Dominic. Let me put you on speaker so my brother can hear you."

Dominic Benedetti.

I resume my seat. Amadeo sets the phone on the coffee table.

"I have good news and bad news," he says. "You have a preference which I start with?"

"Not really," Amadeo says. "Shoot."

"Smart to put a tail on Brady. Probably saved the old man's life."

"Is that the good or bad part?" I ask.

Dominic chuckles, and my brother snorts. "He had a run-in with the brother."

"Lucien? You have him?" Amadeo asks, sitting up and leaning toward the phone.

"That's the bad news. No. He slipped away. I have men looking, but he's gone."

"Where were they?"

"Just outside a private club in the city. Brady was... indulging in the entertainment, shall we say, when the host approached to let him know there was a call for him. He excused himself, and we found him exiting through the kitchen to the alley. Never a good idea when dealing with crooks."

"You'd think he'd know that by now," I say.

"We had eyes on him almost immediately. Lucien met him there, and they talked for a few minutes. Things got heated when he saw Lucien came armed."

"Go on."

"He attacked Brady before my soldier could stop him and, in the chaos, ran."

"Any of your soldiers hurt?" Amadeo asks.

"No, they're fine."

"Brady?"

"Flesh wound but you wouldn't know it to hear him whine."

I roll my eyes.

"Found it interesting that Russo had a black eye. Someone beat him but not too badly."

"An incentive beating," Amadeo says.

"I think so. Nothing was broken as far as my men could see."

"I'm going to guess that's the Russians, and they want payment for their dead soldiers. Where's Brady?"

"Home. I'm texting you his address now. My men will be waiting for you."

"Thanks, Dominic. We owe you."

"It's good to have allies around the world. You never know when you might need them." Translation, we will be repaying the favor, which is fine by me.

Amadeo disconnects the call. I'm already on my feet putting my jacket on as he's tucking the phone into his pocket and grabbing his blazer. We ride the elevator impatiently to the garage to pick up the SUV, and Amadeo enters the address into the GPS as I pull out into traffic.

The good and bad thing with this city is it really doesn't sleep. It's close to one in the morning and traffic to the old man's posh neighborhood is still a bitch. Given that and the location, it takes us over an hour to get there. When we do, we park behind two other SUVs along the circular drive of the mansion set far enough back into its own property that it would be one of those houses that, when we were little, Dad would say something like "if you can't see it from the road, we can't afford it."

Dominic's men open the front door as we approach and direct us up to the second floor. Amadeo and I walk side by side up the wide staircase.

"His job pays well," I comment.

"I'm sure it's all that not working with crooks."

We hear him before we even get to the one door that's guarded.

"I need to get to a hospital. I need a real doctor."

Amadeo and I exchange a look and enter the large bedroom where the old man is sitting on the edge of the bed, his shirt off as someone sticks a bandage onto his side. When he sees us, he doesn't show surprise. I think he may have aged ten years tonight. He looks frail with his narrow shoulders, his caved-in chest, and small but soft, round belly. Sparse, white hair dots both chest and stomach, and I think about Dominic's comment that he was indulging in the entertainment. Did some poor woman have to touch that?

When Brady's eyes land on us, he goes silent.

"Heard you had a run-in with my brother-in-law," Amadeo says.

The man attending to Brady backs away as Brady tilts his chin up and doesn't bother to respond.

"How bad is it?" Amado asks the soldier.

"Surface. It's already stopped bleeding."

"I need a proper doctor," Brady insists.

I walk over to touch the wound, poke at it. He winces. I peel back the bandage and take in the cut. Like Dominic said, it's a surface wound. I press the bandage back in place.

"It could use some disinfectant. Have any alcohol?" I ask him. "It'll sting but..."

His eyes grow huge.

"We'll get you to a doctor after you answer a few

questions," Amadeo says.

I take a look around at all his things. "This is almost as nice as our place," I say. "Really pay this well, your job? You only worked for the Russo family, as far as I'm aware."

"Where's Lucien Russo?" Amadeo asks him.

"He did this to me. How the hell would I know?"

"Question is why did he do it to you?" I ask.

He clams up.

"I, too, am very curious about why," Amadeo starts. "Knowing Benedetti's men and my own are looking for him, why would he come out of hiding to see you? What makes you so special?"

Crickets.

My phone vibrates with a call. It's Bruno, so I excuse myself while Amadeo continues to question him. I assume he's going to tell me they landed safely and Vittoria is secured in Ravello. I hope that's what he's going to say. But the timing makes me anxious.

"Bruno?" I say as I close the bedroom door behind me. "All good?"

"Yes, all is fine. Vittoria is at the Ravello house. I forgot to text you when we landed, but I was pretty engrossed."

"Engrossed with what?"

"That lawyer, Brady, he got a hell of a bonus about six years ago around the time the will was changed."

"Oh?"

"A transfer was initiated by Geno Russo literally days before Vittoria was admitted to that quack's clinic.

But it's not only that. There are other transfers of money. Sizeable amounts. These are classified the same way as the transfers to Dmitri Anders. They're the only ones classified this way."

"What are you thinking?"

"Brady wasn't surprised when the Russian team came into the offices to 'arrest' you. He didn't seem at all nervous even. I remember finding that strange. It's almost as though he expected it."

"You think he's working with Lucien?"

"Might be. I just sent you the files. The transactions are highlighted."

"Your timing is impeccable, Bruno. We were just paying the old man a visit after Lucien attacked him. I guess their partnership was headed south."

"You found the brother then?"

"No. He slipped away."

"Well, Ravello is secured. You don't have to worry about that. I'll be heading up there in the morning to check on things. When will you be back?"

"Hoping tomorrow. I guess it depends on our chat with the old man now."

"Keep me posted."

"Will do. Thanks, Bruno."

"Welcome."

I head back into the bedroom to find my brother with his arms folded across his chest and an irritated look on his face. I open the file and take in the amounts.

"Did Geno Russo pay you to cover up the killing of

Vittoria's rapists, or were you working with Lucien to hire the bastards?"

I'm not sure who is more surprised when they turn toward me, Brady or my brother.

"That was Bruno," I tell Amadeo. "Judging from the bonuses he was paid, Mr. Brady was a model employee." I share the figures with Amadeo, who whistles through his teeth. "First one looks like was authorized by Geno. A six-figure 'bonus.' Is that normal?"

Brady clears his throat.

"What happened to the righteous 'I won't work with crooks' part?" I ask.

"Mr. Russo wasn't a crook." He stands to reach for his shirt.

"Sit," Amadeo says.

"I'd like to get dressed."

"And I'd like some answers. Sit."

He takes a good look at my brother then at me and parks his old ass back down.

"I meant what I said about Vittoria. That girl doesn't deserve to have anything else happen to her. She's been through hell."

"Just to be sure we're on the same page, you're talking about the kidnapping, imprisonment, and rape, am I right?" Amadeo asks.

His mouth falls open.

"What was your part in it?" I ask.

"How do you know about that?" he asks, voice quieter.

"Met with Doc Tilbury," Amadeo says. "Did you

know he keeps a video of each session?"

He doesn't respond to that.

"Back to your role, though. What did you do exactly for the bonus?" Amadeo asks.

"You helped to get rid of the bodies?" I suggest.

"That's not exactly my area."

"No, that's right. You don't work with criminals."

"I did it for the child. I made that scum disappear, so as far as the world was concerned, the bastards never existed. Geno took care of getting rid of any physical evidence."

"Including the bodies."

He nods.

"And he paid you a hefty sum."

He hesitates before he nods, and Amadeo and I exchange a look.

"What?" I ask.

"Nothing."

"Let me get the alcohol to clean that wound," I say, walking toward the bathroom.

"Wait. I don't know why I would even cover this up anymore."

"Go on," Amadeo says calmly.

"Lucien arranged it. What happened to her was Lucien's doing."

It takes my brother and I both a minute to digest that even though on some level we knew.

"He told you that? Geno Russo? I'm guessing Lucien didn't exactly come to beg forgiveness."

"He suspected, then found out for sure. There was

a money trail."

"Always is. What about these other payments made to you?" I ask.

"The father was afraid of his son," he says. "He should have cut Lucien off, but he was too much a coward and only did it after his own death. He left that girl in danger if you ask me."

He looks at us as if expecting us to agree with him, which I do, and I'm sure my brother does too, but the old man is an opportunist. He is no ally of ours.

"Continue," Amadeo says. "Explain why Lucien made those other payments to you."

"Hell, maybe it'll shed some light on who Dmitri Anders is," I add.

He pales.

"You know the name. We'll come back to that. The payments," Amadeo says.

"I told Lucien I knew he had set his sister up. I threatened to turn him in to the authorities or, at the very least, tell his father. He wasn't aware that his father already knew and had already acted. All he knew was that there would be repercussions if Geno ever learned the truth."

"And Lucien believed you that Geno didn't know."

The old man nods.

"Wiley, I'll give you that. Weren't you afraid one or both would find out you were playing both sides?"

He shrugs a shoulder. "Geno trusted me, and I knew I could manage Lucien."

"With friends like you, you don't need enemies. Is

that the expression?" I ask.

He gives me a nasty look.

"Turns out you couldn't manage Lucien, though," Amadeo says. "What happened tonight?"

"He thought to put an end to our agreement."

"To you blackmailing him, you mean, considering he figured out you've been playing him for years at the reading of the will."

"I could always make the disappeared men reappear," the old man says.

"You're very talented then, Mr. Brady."

"Lucien is an animal. Any man who can do to his sister what he had done to her is an animal."

"A point we agree on." Amadeo steps right up to him. "You're not going to breathe a word of any of this to anyone. I don't ever want Vittoria finding out or remembering."

"She won't remember. Dr. Tilbury's methods are sound."

"I hope you're right. Where would Lucien have gone?"

He shakes his head. "I wasn't exactly a confidant of his, but I do know if he's smart, he'll be running from Dmitri Anders. Unless, of course, he found some way to repay him. I'm sure Anders would take a different sort of payment."

I bristle.

He grins. "Keep her safe. If her brother gets to her... Well, let's just say you don't want her brother to get to her."

## 20

## VITTORIA

I can't keep my eyes open, but every time I drift off with that leatherbound book on my lap, I dream of Hannah. Hannah and Lucien. I'm running out of time. I need to devise a plan and find some way to get Emma, Hyacinth, and me out of here. I can't leave Hyacinth behind. I won't abandon her after all she's done for us. And I'm sure if I did, the brothers would use her to bait me back. I have cash. I have access to my bank account. And I have the phone. But it's all useless without a single contact on the outside.

Although, I do have one contact. Lucien. He can get us out and plant us firmly in Sonny Caballero's control. Sonny hates Amadeo and Bastian, and I know in my gut that he would just use us to get what he wants from them. To hurt them. In that case, isn't it better to stay here? To trust Amadeo and Bastian?

No. I can't trust them. They're not trustworthy, not when it comes to our freedom. They say they want to keep us safe, and while I believe they mean that, being a prisoner is not safe. Especially not when the men holding you have powerful enemies. Emma and I are pawns. We are, as Amadeo very clearly stated what feels like a decade ago, collateral damage. But are we expendable? There is something between the brothers and me. I feel it. I know they do, too. On some level, I do trust them. They won't hurt us. But as long as we are here, we are not free.

I set the book aside and reach into my bag for the photo I took from the penthouse. The one of Mom and me I found in dad's desk drawer. He used to have it on top but had put it away at some point. I don't really remember when that happened.

I haven't shown it to Emma. I don't want to upset her. I look at the photo. It's old, but it's one of my favorites. She looks happy here. She's beautiful. She was more than a decade younger than Dad. On the frame, it says "my girls" in fancy cursive lettering.

Curious about where it was taken, I slip it out of its frame. I had taken the whole thing so it wouldn't bend in my bag. I set the frame aside and turn the photo over to read Portland, Oregon. I remember that trip. Mom had wanted to visit the town she'd been born in even though no relatives remained there. Under Portland is the date it was taken, but then, beneath that and written in black Sharpie, is a website link along with what looks like a password. It's Dad's writing but not his usual elegant style. These are block letters. Angry-looking block letters.

I switch my phone on, and when it finds a signal, I hit the Safari icon and enter the address, noticing how my heartbeat has sped up and hearing that warning in my head that I shouldn't do this, shouldn't look. I sit up as the website loads to show a black background with a box opening up at the center, the cursor resting there. It's all very ominous. Taking the code from the back of the photo, a random string of letters and numbers, I type it in, and a part of me wishes it won't work. Wishes I'll get an error message or something. But then the screen changes, and from the black background, a bright, happy, almost maniacally so, smiley face appears, starting out small, then growing large enough to fill the entire screen. It hovers there and makes me shudder.

And then I see the first image.

For a moment, I'm not sure what I'm looking at. Or maybe I don't want to know what it is. But I click through, as if on autopilot, to scroll to the next one. And the next one. And the ones after that. My hand goes to my mouth as my brain processes what I'm seeing.

My mother.

My mother with a man who is not my father.

The photos begin to blur as my eyes fill with tears, and masochist that I am, I keep clicking only to see more and more photos of them together. My mother and her lover. A man whose face I never see. A man who is very clearly not my father, not with his build, not with those tattoos.

Dad's letter to me comes to mind. The betrayal he'd felt. My conversation with Bastian and Amadeo telling me Emma isn't my father's daughter repeats itself, their voices so clear. I see the evidence they had. And then I hear what Lucien said. How Dad wasn't surprised about the accident that killed her. That almost killed my sister. My sister who won't speak and is terrified of men.

And tears spill from my eyes as I remember the man I knew. The one who loved me. Only me. The one who put this photo of his girls where he wouldn't have to see it day in and day out. Who, by the end, couldn't stand to look at Mom if I'm being honest. And Mom, who, by the end, cowered from him. It all makes sense, I think, as I look down onto the small screen of my phone and see Mom's face, see Mom in the arms of a stranger. Mom happy. It all fits.

The library door opens, and I jump, quickly dropping the phone into my bag and standing, wiping my eyes, looking as guilty as I feel. It's Hyacinth, and she startles. I don't know if it's because she found me in here or the state I'm in.

"Vittoria. Are you okay? Has something happened?"

I wipe my eyes and shake my head. "No, it's fine. I'm fine." I look behind her for Emma but she's alone.

"I told Emma I'd look for you to read to her. She was up early and upset you weren't there when she woke up."

"God. Of course, she was. I didn't even realize the time. I'll go right up."

"I'll get us some coffee and meet you up there. She's setting her stuffed animals and dolls up for a tea party. All of them." She rolls her eyes but is smiling warmly.

I love the innocence of the act. "Thanks, Hyacinth."

She nods even though she looks worried. I give her hand a squeeze and head up to Emma's bedroom as she disappears into the kitchen.

But as I'm approaching her bedroom door, I hear it. The chopper landing. They're back. I'm out of time. I hurry into Emma's room and find her at the window, watching as the chopper lands. It's so stark and loud against the peaceful backdrop of the sun rising. But it's what I see, or more who I see, spilling out of the chopper that silences me, that has me grabbing Emma's hand hard as, from downstairs, we hear the sounds of men. A lot of men. And gunfire.

Because it's not the brothers who have returned. These are soldiers.

I turn to Emma and see the tea party she was preparing in the large walk-in closet. See all the stuffed animals taking up the entire back wall.

"Hide," I tell her. She's good at that. Has been since Mom died. "Go. Hide." I rush into the closet with her even as I hear footsteps charging up the stairs. "And don't come out until someone you know and trust comes to get you. Do you understand? Me or Hyacinth. Understand?" She nods, but she looks terrified. "Bastian or Amadeo," I add at the last minute. She's squeezing my hand so tight I'm not sure she'll let go. "No one else. No one!"

She nods, too frightened to even cry. I'm grateful for her silence for the first time ever as she does as I say, and I rush out of the closet and close the door just as soldiers burst into the bedroom.

## 21

## BASTIAN

Our flight is landing when the call comes in, and even though it's not the middle of the night or in any way unusual for Bruno to be calling at eight in the morning, I know before I answer that something is wrong.

Amadeo and I descend the stairs of the jet and step onto the tarmac. The chopper that will take us up to Ravello is waiting in the distance.

"Bruno?" I ask as I slide the green bar across the screen to accept the call.

"You land?" he asks, voice tight.

"Just now. What is it?" Amadeo and I both stop. I put the phone on speaker and bring it close to our ears, given the noise.

"You need to get to Ravello."

"What's happened?"

"We were attacked."

My heart stops.

"Your mother is okay," he says. "I'm with her now."

I wait. So does Amadeo. I don't think either of us wants to ask the question.

"Francesca was killed. As was the nanny."

I'm not breathing.

"Vittoria and Emma are gone."

Gone?

Gone is good, right?

Gone is better than dead.

"Mom wasn't hurt?"

"No, but she's upset. Very upset. I'm afraid she might have witnessed the killings."

"We're on our way," Amadeo says.

I disconnect the call and push the phone into my pocket as we run to the chopper. We're barely strapped in, headsets on, as the pilot takes off, and I dig my phone out of my pocket.

Me: *Jarno?*

Bruno: *Badly injured. He won't make it. It's a fucking massacre. I've alerted our men in Naples, and a few are on their way here.*

I show the phone to Amadeo so he can read the text.

I look at Amadeo. "We need to move her."

"Agree. I'll make a call as soon as we land. Call in another favor."

"Who?"

"Stefan Sabbioni. We'll send her to Sicily."

We sit in tense silence, the chopper flying too slowly. When it finally lands in Ravello, we're both running across the lawn toward the back entrance of the house. I can already see the carnage, the blood on the furniture Mom loves to sit on to look out at the garden as she has her tea in the afternoons. The knocked over chairs. The downed men.

Amadeo makes the call, keeping it brief. Two men who are usually stationed at the Naples house emerge armed with automatic rifles slung over their chests. They're wearing protective gear like they're ready for war.

Bruno walks out behind them, his face grave.

"Where's Mom?" I ask.

"Doctor just gave her a sedative. She's in her room. Go see her. She'll feel better when she sees your faces."

We nod, and both go upstairs, taking in the destruction of the house—the walls riddled with bullets, the glass shards of the windows on the stained marble floor. Armed soldiers stand at the front doors and at every window.

Mom's room is at the far end. I notice the open door of Emma's bedroom and stop to pick up the stuffed pig she'd been carrying that day I took her from the shrink's office. I pick it up as we walk to Mom's bedroom, and I see Amadeo's eyes move to the closed door of Vittoria's room. The one she was locked in when we first took her. Before she was anything to us other than the enemy.

Vittoria is safe for now, as is Emma. They could have killed them along with the rest and left their bodies for us to find. But they didn't. They're alive.

"Mom?" Amadeo says as we walk in. Her doctor is standing beside the bed, and a nurse is adjusting the blankets.

"The sedative I gave her is strong," the doctor says, moving away as we approach the bed where Mom opens her eyes and reaches out a hand. I take it.

"Mom." I brush her hair back from her face. She looks up at me, then at Amadeo and takes his hand too.

"They didn't get you," she says, drawing us closer. "They didn't get you."

"No, we're okay, Mom. You go to sleep now. We'll talk about it when you wake up."

"Francesca," she says, and tears roll down her face.

"Shh. Close your eyes, Mom. Go to sleep." She does because of the sedative, and we turn to the doctor.

"She's physically all right."

"Thank you, Doctor," Amadeo says. "We're moving her. You and the nurse will go with her?" Although he asks it as a question, it's not.

The doctor glances at the woman who nods. "Of course."

"Your cell phones, Doctor."

He raises his eyebrows.

"For her safety."

He hands over his phone and turns to the nurse who does the same.

"Thank you," I say.

Bruno is waiting for us in the doorway. "Naples?"

"No. Sicily. Stefan Sabbioni will house her until this is done," Amadeo says.

"I'll arrange transport."

"Where's Francesca's body?"

"In the kitchen. She and Hyacinth are both there. They were surprised, I think. It would have been quick."

I nod because I don't trust myself to speak.

"Jarno?"

He shakes his head. "He was in the library."

Amadeo mutters a curse under his breath.

"And Vittoria and Emma aren't here," I say. It's not a question.

"You're sure? You searched everywhere?" Amadeo asks.

"Everywhere. I got here about an hour ago to find the carnage. Called in men. We searched the house and the grounds. No trace of them."

"Find out where my uncle is," Amadeo says as he and I walk into Emma's bedroom to find it torn apart, like the rest of the house. No bullets here, though. No one was killed in here. I set the little well-loved pig on the bed. The closet door is open, and I see the tea party they must have been having. Someone kicked the tiny cups over and the icing from the cake is embedded in the carpet. I crouch down to see the heavy tread of the boot's imprint.

I stand, look over the stuffed animals. There are

dozens in various sizes along with baby and Barbie dolls strewn in. I turn to go when my gaze lands on Emma's torn-apart little shoes. She always put them on the minute she got out of bed.

Amadeo lays a hand on my shoulder "We'll get them back," he says. "He took them. He wants something in exchange, or he'd have killed them and left them for us to find."

I nod. I know that.

"I want to have a look at the other bedrooms," he says.

I follow him and am almost to the door when I hear a sound. It's so soft I almost doubt that I heard anything at all, but I stop and listen. It's quiet, unnaturally still. Graveyard still. Amadeo leaves, but something tells me to wait. A full minute passes before I hear it again. It's so quiet it's almost nothing. Not quite a whisper. Almost not noise at all. I take my pistol and cock it as I turn back into the room.

Not many places to hide. I can see under the beds from where I am. No one's under there. Not that a soldier would be hiding under a bed. The bathroom door is ajar, and I push it fully open. No one's behind the shower curtain. No one's here at all. I walk inside and open the cabinet under the sink, feeling stupid for looking there, but I do it, and it's empty. Which makes me feel stupider.

I straighten, shake my head, and cross the room to the door when it comes again, and this time I stop and turn to look into the closet with its still-open door. I cock my head as I take in the array of stuffed animals and dolls. And I hear it again. I step toward the pile and re-engage the Glock's safety before pushing it into its holster. And this time when I hear the sound, I think I can make out a word.

*Help.*

My heart races as I crouch down to push the animals out of the way, and I almost don't believe it when I see a cloud of curly blond hair, then big brown eyes. Big, terrified brown eyes that stare up at me, her scarred face streaked with tears. She's moving her mouth, muttering one word. Trying to make a sound.

"Help."

Relief like I've never felt floods my system. It's a moment of light as Emma reaches out to me. I take her in my arms and feel her tiny body press into mine as her arms put a stranglehold around my neck.

"Emma," I say, standing, carrying the little thing with me as she sobs quiet tears into my neck and keeps trying to say that one word.

"Help. Help. Help."

I walk out of the closet and sit on the edge of her bed. She's holding on to me so tightly that it takes effort to draw her back far enough to see her face. I wipe her eyes and try to offer a reassuring smile.

"I heard you, Emma," I say. "I can hear you."

She hugs me, then reaches for something. The pig. It's just out of reach so I grab it for her and look her over, make sure she's unharmed. She is.

"You hid well," I tell her.

"Vittoria," she says, the sound so quiet it's not even a whisper. "Vittoria is gone. Bad man. Bad." And she starts to sob all over again, her body wracked with it. I wrap a hand over the back of her head and draw her to me, standing as I do.

"We're going to get Vittoria back," I tell her as I walk out of the room, keeping my hand on her head so her face is buried against my neck. I don't want her to see the carnage.

A part of my brain is telling me I'm making a promise I may not be able to keep, but I tell that part to shut the fuck up and walk past the open door of Vittoria's empty stripped-down bedroom to Amadeo's. He's sitting on the bed on the side he doesn't sleep on. Vittoria's side now, when she sleeps in his bed. And in his hands, he's holding her tank top, the one with teapots on it. He has it pressed to his nose.

"Look who I found," I say.

Amadeo stiffens, and he stands with his back to me for a moment. I think he's composing himself. When he turns to us and sees Emma, a wide smile spreads across his face.

"Emma." He comes to her, rubbing her back and patting her hair. She looks at him, then at the tank top.

"Vittoria," she says, reaching a hand to the tank top. I meet my brother's eyes over the top of her head. His face is set, hard, that smile vanished. It's the way he looked before, in the beginning. As we plotted our revenge.

"We will get Vittoria back," he tells Emma in a voice I barely recognize. But I understand why. Because we will get her back. Just not sure in what state.

## 22

## VITTORIA

I got the soldiers out of the bedroom as fast as I could. I didn't struggle more than I had to to show that I was struggling. I just needed them gone. They wanted us both. They searched for her, but they were in a hurry to leave. I knew why once we were on the chopper. An entourage was headed to the villa. Amadeo and Bastian? Had they flown through the night and were arriving just this morning? What a scene would greet them.

My mind wandered to Hyacinth, Nora, and Francesca. Did they spare them? Because they had shot every guard dead.

At least Emma is safe. They'll find her. I just hope they do it before she comes out of her hiding place. She can't see what those soldiers left behind.

The chopper carries us near to Naples and once it touches down, the soldiers I'm riding with drag me out. I keep my head low as I run with them. They put a blindfold on me and have my wrists bound behind my back so I will fall flat on my face if they let me go.

Car doors open and shut. I'm shoved into the back of a low vehicle and sandwiched inside by a soldier on either side of me. We drive for about an hour, maybe more. I can't see through the blindfold, but all the city noise is gone by the time the car stops. When they haul me out, my arms scream at the angle. I trip over some stairs, but they keep me upright, and soon, I'm indoors.

"Downstairs," a man says, and I tense as I'm half-carried through the house and down a set of stairs to a space too cold to be above ground. It takes all I have to keep the panic from overtaking me. I try to think of Emma. I saved Emma. That's the most important part. I just need to focus on that.

Once we're down, my captors force me onto a chair and unlock my wrists to re-bind them to the chair itself. They do the same with my ankles, spreading my legs and cuffing each to a chair-leg. And I wonder if I'm just destined to die in a rank, old basement. I may have escaped fate before, but now it's finally caught me.

Footsteps clomp heavily up and away, and it's quiet. That's when I hear it. *Tick. Tick. Tick.* A clock.

My breathing becomes ragged as an image flashes across my eyelids. Another clock. Another basement. The cold steel of handcuffs. The weight of chains.

*Tick.*

*Tick.*

I hated that clock. I fucking hated it.

A touch at the back of my head draws me out of my head, and I gasp.

I'm not alone.

I feel a tug, and the blindfold slips away. I blink, opening my eyes wide as they adjust. But it's so dark here, pitch black, they may as well be closed.

The man at my back moves, and I turn my head to follow the sound. He's like a shadow and when I look up at his face, I glimpse a skull and almost cry out.

It's a mask. Just a mask.

"Where am I?" I ask as he walks confidently in this pitch-black. He knows his way around. That ticking of the clock continues. "Where the fuck am I?" I demand as he ascends the stairs.

Nothing.

The door opens. Light shines down momentarily, and I see the white face of the clock set in front of me. There are things stuck to the wall just beneath the clock. But I can't make them out. The door closes too quickly, plunging me into darkness again, that clock my only companion. For a moment, as my heart pounds against my chest and I look around at all the blackness and feel the cold of the basement penetrate my bones as that clock ticks with hateful efficiency, I think this can't get worse.

But it does.

And darkness isn't the worst thing at all.

The lights blink on and off, and on and off, bright fluorescent unnatural light, and I wish he'd left the blindfold on as, during those bursts of light, I see what's on that wall beneath that goddamned clock. Fucking plastered across the length of the room. And those lights. Fuck. The lights won't stop blinking. I twist and turn in my chair and try to free myself, but I can't get out. I can't get away. I couldn't then. And I can't now.

I scream.

## 23

## AMADEO

Bastian will take Mom and Emma to Palermo. I won't join them. I have something I need to take care of. Something I should have taken care of long ago. Because what happened lies squarely on my shoulders.

I sit in the back seat with two soldiers in the front as we drive to my uncle's Naples apartment, a luxury unit in a renovated old building in the heart of town. The video footage of what took place in the hours before our landing replays in my mind. A chopper landing. Soldiers unloading. A truckload of them arriving at the same time at the front gates as the first chopper took off, and a second landed, unloading more men.

The house was secured. We had plenty of soldiers. But they had more, and they took us by surprise. They came ready to kill.

Our men killed three of theirs, but the tally of dead

on our side is much higher.

The hardest part to bear, though, is the footage at the end. After the truck full of soldiers drove back down the hill. It's the image of Vittoria half dragged out of the house by two men easily twice her size. That image of Vittoria disappearing into the chopper.

"Sir?"

I blink, then look at the man in the passenger seat who is turned halfway around to talk to me.

"We're a block out," he says.

I look out at the neighborhood and nod. "Go to the building."

He raises his eyebrows, surprised.

"I said go to the building." This isn't some incognito mission. I want Sonny to see me coming.

A few minutes later, we're parked in front of the building. The doorman opens the doors, and I cross the large lobby. It's like a fucking hotel, an exclusive address for the wealthiest of the wealthy in the city.

Two soldiers, Sonny's because as far as I know he's the only mobster living at this address, stop us when we get to the elevator. They're dressed in suits with their weapons out of sight.

"Get the fuck out of my way," I tell the one.

He looks at me, then at my men. "You can go up but no soldiers." I guess Sonny's expecting me. "Arms out."

I take my weapon out of its shoulder holster and hand it to one of my men, then let the two pat me down. One is already alerting Sonny we're on our way as the other rides up with me. I stare straight ahead barely seeing my own face in the reflection of the gold-tinted mirror on the doors.

When we arrive on the top floor, the doors slide open, and two more men are waiting at the entrance to Sonny's apartment. It's one of two on this floor.

"He's clean," the man who rode up with me says as the other two stand aside, and I enter. Another soldier acknowledges me with a nod and escorts me toward Sonny's office, set in the farthest room down the corridor. Once we reach the door, he opens it and steps aside to let me enter. My uncle, his face still bruised, the swelling around his eye not quite completely gone, sits in the center of the leather sofa, looking fucking ecstatic as he leans back and folds his arms across his chest. Two men stand nearby.

"Nephew," he says in that grating way he has.

"Where is my wife?"

"How the fuck would I know?" His smug grin tells me he does know. He looks me over. "You look a little worse for wear."

I'm sure I do. I barely slept on the flight back and am wearing the same clothes. But I could give a fuck. I reach into the breast pocket of my suit jacket, and Sonny's expression changes quickly as his men step forward, drawing their weapons.

I ignore them, take out the older model phone, and scroll to what I need.

They relax.

"You need me to buy you a new phone, nephew? That looks like it's from the last century."

"Not quite but it is old," I tell him. "The Reaper only had one use for it."

My uncle's face pales as he glances at his soldiers.

"My wife," I say.

He looks at me with such contempt, it's a palpable thing.

"As with the earlier attack on her, it wasn't me. You'd do better to spend your time tracking down the brother. I hear he flew in recently."

I make sure he can't see any change in my expression, but I am fucking surprised. Lucien is in Italy?

"So you had nothing to do with the attack at the villa," I say more a comment than a question and he shakes his head with that too-smug grin on his too-smug face. He's lying. And he wants me to know it. That's why mom wasn't hurt. That was his calling card.

"Even if I did, I am the rightful heir."

"This isn't a fucking kingdom."

"The family would support me."

"You know the death warrant stands on the man who killed Angelo even though Grandfather is dead," I remind him.

I see the infinitesimal change come over his expression.

"I'm going to ask you one more time. Where is my wife?"

"And I'm going to tell you one more time you should ask her brother," he says, standing to move out of the way as he signals to the soldiers. Before they get to me, I hit play on the phone, and Sonny's voice rings out, always recognizable, as he strikes a deal with The Reaper to assassinate his own son. And in the moment that the soldiers hesitate as they hear the recording, I reach into my boot and take Vittoria's pretty little knife, advancing on my uncle and plunging it into his gut as I pull him to me, driving the blade to its hilt and hearing the gurgling sound of him choking on his blood.

I tug his head backward, draw the knife up to slice his gut and look him in the eye as I do it, as, in the background, he laughs as the deal is struck, the date agreed.

"Bastian was right. I should have done this years ago," I say and thrust him away, letting his body fall onto the couch, then slump to the floor. I turn to the soldiers who look beyond me to Sonny's body. "Get the word out. Sonny Caballero is dead. Anyone who wants to join me is welcome. Anyone who stands against me will meet with the same end Sonny just did."

## 24

## BASTIAN

After settling my mother and Emma in Palermo, I go straight to Uncle's apartment in the city. Word is breaking about what Amadeo has done. Bruno is already here and waiting upstairs, and there are more soldiers than I've seen gathered at one house since the death of our grandfather. The elevator is blocked by our men. I ride up, and once the doors open to Sonny's floor, I see half a dozen soldiers armed with automatic rifles standing in the hall.

Eyebrows raised, I bypass them, enter, and am directed to Sonny's study, where I find Bruno. He's the one who called and alerted me to what happened. What my brother did. I'm only sorry I wasn't there to see the life bleed out of that bastard's eyes myself.

Bruno is on a call. I nod in greeting and walk over to where Sonny's body is splayed half on the floor, half on the sofa. I lift the blanket covering him and whistle at the amount of blood.

"New bag?" Bruno comments.

I cover the body and turn to him. I'm carrying Vittoria's tote, which I'd found in the library. I set it down.

"Vittoria's. Where is Amadeo?"

"Sent him to take a shower."

"Find anything on Vittoria's location?"

Bruno shakes his head. "Not yet but I've been busy trying to head off the cops."

"Word travels fast," Amadeo says from the door.

I turn to find my brother standing fresh from a shower, hair still wet dressed casually in jeans and a dark sweater. I'm guessing Bruno had the forethought to bring a change of clothes. Amadeo glances at the body, then at me.

"How are Mom and Emma?"

"Fine. Good call to send them to Palermo. Emma took to Gabriela right away."

"Good."

"You are aware there's a warrant out for your arrest," Bruno tells Amadeo.

"Yeah, well, that's all going to have to wait until I've found my wife." Amadeo settles himself behind the desk.

"You need to get out of here," Bruno says, ignoring him.

"Any luck with the password?" Amadeo asks him.

"Not yet."

"Try Nadia," I say more as a joke than anything else.

Amadeo chuckles. "Well, fuck. I'd say that's brilliant, but quite frankly, it was more idiotic of Sonny than anything else."

"It worked? You're fucking kidding me," I say.

Amadeo offers Bruno the seat. What might take my brother or me hours to find Bruno will find in about a third of the time.

I bring the tote over.

"Isn't that Vittoria's bag?" Amadeo asks.

"You really do need to go," Bruno tells Amadeo.

"In a minute."

"Found this," I say, taking out her phone as well as the cash and setting both on the desk.

He shakes his head. "That's our bad. We should have searched what that bastard handed to her. She have contact with anyone?"

"No calls but she did have a conversation over text with her brother. He offered to get her out."

"And?"

"Doesn't seem like she took him up on it at least according to the chat."

"Good."

"But there's something else." I pick up the phone, navigate to Safari, and hand it to Amadeo.

"How did she get these?"

I show him the photo with the website and password. "I'm guessing Lucien handed it to Geno."

"Anything else?"

"Not really."

My phone dings. "That's a list of possible safehouses he'd have taken her to," Bruno says, turning to us. "But you need to go. Now. You won't be much good to anyone sitting in a jail cell."

"That's why I'm counting on you not to let that happen. Sonny has to have something on the officials in his pocket."

"I'm sure he does, but until I find it," Bruno says, putting a flash drive into Sonny's computer and pushing some buttons before turning to face us. "You need to stay out of sight. I'm serious, Amadeo. I need time, and my priority is finding Vittoria. Help me to help you." The computer screen goes black. Bruno takes the drive, pockets it, and stands.

"I'll stay out of sight, but I'm not going into hiding like a fucking coward while Vittoria is out there on her own."

"Bastian?" Bruno turns to me.

"I'm with Amadeo on this one."

He shakes his head. "Let's go," he says.

I open the folder on my phone. "There are two dozen addresses in here."

"I'll try to narrow it down," he says as he searches for something in the wall.

"What are you doing?" Amadeo asks.

"Sonny had an exit plan in case things ever went south." Something pops, and a part of the wall springs open. "And here it is. It'll take you down to the garage. Car is waiting. Keep your phones on."

Amadeo looks at him, nods. "Thank you." He then turns to me. "What about Mom and Emma? If anything happens to me—"

"I'm going with you, brother."

"Someone needs to be there in case—"

"Nothing's going to happen," I say again. "We go together. Period."

"And I'll be there," Bruno adds, then turns to me. "Get him out of here."

## 25

## VITTORIA

My throat is hoarse, and I'm lying on the floor on my side, still cuffed to the chair, losing my fucking mind when the lights finally stop flickering and go out, plunging me into utter darkness.

For a moment, everything stops. But then that clock ticks, and I hear myself repeating the same words over and over. Muttering them. It's the language of the insane.

My left arm has gone numb, and my cheekbone throbs. I'm lying with my full weight on my arm, and my face hit the concrete floor when I toppled. I don't remember it happening, though. Can't remember when I fell over. All I know is what I kept seeing. The gruesome images plastered to the walls. I don't know if it was the same one or not. Blood and brains and the inside of someone's head.

I squeeze my eyes shut against the nausea that makes my stomach spasm. I'm not struggling. I stopped a while ago. I'm lying here instead remembering the endless ticking of another clock. The blinking of another set of lights.

The smell of bleach permeates my nostrils, and although I know it's not real, I swear I can still feel the burn as I scrubbed my hands raw. But it was either that or blood.

Suddenly, the light blinks on. It's blindingly bright and jolts me from my thoughts. My eyelids fly open, and I stare straight ahead at the images stuck to the wall. A whine that doesn't sound like me comes from deep inside my belly, and I close my eyes, even as I hear the footsteps descending. Even as I know my assailant is coming for me. I keep them closed when he stops within inches of me. I don't want to look. I can't see. Because what if that's not all I see? What more is plastered to those walls?

"Shit," a man mutters. I know the voice, but I keep my eyes sealed shut as the chair is abruptly righted. Pins and needles prick my arm making it sting as blood begins to circulate. All the while, I keep my head down so I don't see those photos.

"Vittoria," the voice says.

I shake my head. "What doesn't kill you makes you stronger, princess." I say it again, realizing what it is I'm muttering, the words I'm repeating in an endless, mad loop.

Princess. I was my dad's princess. And then this happened to me. A basement. Me in a cage. Me on a mattress. The cage was better. They didn't touch me when I was locked in that cage. I remember the smell of it. Of them. Old sweat. Cigarettes. Beer. Fear.

No. That last one was my smell, the fear. They should bottle it. It's an aphrodisiac to some men.

I can still feel their hands on me now. Mouths kissing me. Them inside me.

"Vittoria," the voice says again. There's an urgency in his tone, and this time, he's crouching down in front of me, slapping my face lightly. Amadeo slapped me that night in the basement. Was I muttering the same words then, too?

He was inside me when I took his gun. Moving. Grunting. Taking what I didn't give.

His body felt so heavy on top of me that I almost couldn't breathe. He was still inside me even after he wasn't moving anymore. When he wasn't breathing anymore. I don't think the splatter on the walls was his, though. It was the other one. The one watching, recording my rape on his phone. Something to jerk off to later, I guess. There was no later for him, though. And I smashed that phone against the wall until it lay in so many pieces no one would ever be able to see what was on it.

"Fuck, Vittoria!"

I blink and look at the man crouching down in front of me, his head coming into focus and then blurring out again. Dark eyes, almost black. Dark blond hair. His beard is growing, and it's grayer than it was. Although it's been a while since I've seen his beard because he's always clean-shaven.

"Snap out of it," he says, taking my face with both hands and making me look at him. "We have to get out of here."

"What doesn't kill you," I start, then stop because suddenly I can't remember what comes next.

"Christ. Focus. We need to get the hell out of here. Do you fucking hear me?" Lucien asks. "Where's Emma?"

Emma? Why is he asking about Emma?

"Emma?" I call for her, looking around the basement, trying to blur the images in my periphery. "Emma?" I try again.

"She's not down here," he says irritably. "Where is she?" He unlocks one of the cuffs around my ankles.

I blink, focusing on the top of his head. Has he seen the pictures? Does he know what I did? How can he look so calm?

"Do you see them?" I ask in a voice I don't recognize.

He looks up at me like I'm fucking crazy. "See who?"

I shake my head. "The pictures. On the walls." My voice breaks.

"What pictures?"

"There. On the walls?" I won't look at them, but I gesture with my head.

He looks over, then back at me, and shakes his head. "Jesus. You're fucking losing it. Where's Emma?"

Slowly, I look up. Are they even real? But there they are.

"Vittoria. Fuck. Stop fighting. I can't get these off if you keep moving."

I force a breath in. *What doesn't kill you makes you stronger.* They didn't kill me. I killed them. I'm strong, right?

"Where's Emma, Vittoria?" he asks for the hundredth time.

"Emma." I think as he works on the second ankle. "Hiding. She's hiding. She's safe." I remember.

"She's not safe," he says, and I see how his hair which is usually so well maintained has thinned, how a bald spot is forming. Does he even know he's going bald? I look down at his hands as he unlocks the cuff around my ankle, and I'm hit with a flash of memory. But this one is different than the others. This one isn't gone in an instant like the blinking of those lights. This one, it sticks. The image of hands, mine and his. But last time, they weren't taking the cuffs off. They were putting them on. The ring was there, on the same finger, looking out of place then. Looking out of place now.

I watch his hands work. Clipped nails. Manicured fingers. But I see the dirt under his fingernails.

He moves to the back of the chair to unlock my wrists. "Move," he says, sounding irritated. "We need to go." When I don't move, he pulls me to my feet. My legs feel too wobbly, and my arm is dead weight. I cradle it and follow Lucien to the stairs.

"Where are the soldiers?" I ask, hesitating at the bottom of the staircase as I look up into the room above. We won't get past them. My brother is no fighter, and I don't have a gun.

He glances back. "My men are waiting for us."

I'm confused. We don't have men like those soldiers who took me.

"Let's go."

I stand there and watch him ascend, his hand on the railing. The ring with the insignia like Dad's. It's for the men in our family. A memory takes hold of me, and I have to grab the banister to steady myself as I see that same hand with its ring ascending another set of stairs in another basement in another world leaving me behind. I hear my voice. I'm calling out to him, but he's walking away.

I'm going to be sick. I bring my hands to my head and press the heels of my palms into my eyes. What is happening to me? Am I truly losing my mind?

"Vittoria. What the fuck? We need to move, for fuck's sake. Wait to lose your shit until after this is done, okay?" he says, anxious. His cell phone rings, and he's gone from the basement so I'm alone.

I drop my hands to my sides and open my eyes. The clock ticks, and I make myself look around the room. The single chair. Some paint cans in a corner. Innocuous things.

My heart races as I move my gaze to the walls. I make myself look.

It's the same picture over and over and over again. A dead man. Brains blown out lying facedown on an empty bed. I walk back into the room and right up to the wall. I stare straight at the one in front of me. I reach out a hand and touch it. The photo doesn't vanish into thin air. I rip it from the wall. It's real. It's real. It's in my hands. I fold it into a small square and push it into my pocket.

I walk up the stairs to find my brother talking to one of three men standing outside. I hear one of the strangers speak. He has an accent that's not Italian. Russian, I think.

It must be late afternoon. The light is waning, their shadows growing long. No one else is here, and these men don't look like the ones who took me. They're not dressed the same at least. They all turn to me. Lucien opens the car door and makes a sweeping gesture.

"Ready, princess?" He's irritated.

I walk out of the house, glancing back at it. Just a normal house in a normal neighborhood.

"How did you find me?" I ask.

"I told you I'd get you out. I did. Get in. We have an appointment."

"With who?"

"Whom. With whom."

I stare up at him.

He shakes his head, scratches it. I look at the ring, and I see it on that banister again. Not the one in this house. A different house with a broken banister. Broken stairs.

"With the man who got you out of your prison. Let's fucking go." Out of patience, he takes my arm and shoves me into the car.

## 26

## VITTORIA

We drive for over an hour and all the while I'm thinking, trying to make sense of what's happened. What is happening. Did Amadeo and Bastian arrive at the house? Did they find Emma? I have to believe they have and that she's safe.

I keep glancing at Lucien who must be having a conversation via text as I try to figure this out. I put my hand into my pocket and confirm the photo is there. It's real. Why did he lie about not seeing them?

"Why did you come to Italy?" I ask.

He looks at me. "You give me a hard time when I don't send men after you and then you give me a hard time when I come myself to save your ass." He shifts his attention back to his phone and resumes his furious texting.

I watch out the window, not recognizing anything on roads that seem too far from civilization. It's dark when the driver steers the car onto a narrow, single-lane dirt road, and I watch as we approach what must have once been an old factory. Three large SUVs with windows tinted black are parked outside, and none of this looks good.

"Where are we?" I ask as our car comes to a stop behind the three already there.

Lucien looks straight at me. "Time for you to pull your weight, sis."

"What?"

He climbs out and holds the door open, waiting for me to follow him. I look at the building. It's dark but for a light coming from a room at the far end of the row of windows.

"Out."

"What is this?" I ask, remaining in the car.

He reaches in and grabs my arm to drag me out.

"This is you doing your part for once in your fucking life," he says. I tug to get free, but he slams me backward against the car so hard it knocks the wind out of my lungs. "Did he tell you he changed the will?"

"What?"

"Did he fucking tell you? Were you laughing at me behind my back all along?"

"I don't know what you're talking about. Let me go."

"Did you know all along like that conniving lawyer of his?"

"No. I didn't know anything. Let me go, Lucien."

"I could have let you die, you know that?" he says through his teeth. "I didn't. It was up to me, and I saved your life, and he punished me for it. Everything for his fucking princesses. Always for you and your goddamn mother. Even when he knew what a whore she was."

Those photos come to mind, and he must see that I know something because he grins an ugly grin.

"You know Dad divorced my mother when Leah conveniently got pregnant with you."

Before I can think of an answer, he continues.

"He should have known then once a cheater always a cheater," he says. "She knew I knew," he adds, self-satisfied.

"Knew what?"

The look in his eyes is so strange. Not flat, like it usually is, but an inky black. An unhinged darkness.

"I showed her the pictures. Her spreading her legs for that pig." He grins, gaze moving over me in a way that makes my skin crawl.

"What?" And then I get it. "What did you do?"

"I gave her an out, and like the whore she is, she took it." His eyes go out of focus. It's like he's looking right through me and that grin trembles, then vanishes, and rage takes over. "She shouldn't have laughed at me. That's what cost her in the end." His lip curls, and he blinks several times before he focuses on me. "You look like her, a fucking carbon copy."

I look over his shoulder at the deserted road. "Let me go, Lucien." I stare up at him, unsure how to react, what to say or do. A door clangs and we both turn to find a big guy with shoulders as wide as the doorframe step outside. He has a Glock tucked into his belt. He comes toward us.

I try to wriggle free. Though what am I going to do if I manage to get away from Lucien? Where am I going to run to? And how am I going to get away from the hulk.

"You're keeping him waiting," he says in a Russian accent. "Move," he tells Lucien, then gives him a shove toward the building.

I look up at my half brother. "What is this?"

But he just tugs me along because he's afraid. I see that much in his eyes. That talk of his men was all for show. Now, I see his fear. And fear makes men desperate.

Lucien keeps hold of me as we enter the building, the incredible fucking hulk behind us. As we move deeper inside, dim, naked bulbs light our way

"If you want to keep Emma safe, you just do what I say, understand?" he tells me quietly enough that the hulk won't overhear. "Remember, I can make her life a living hell."

We turn into the next hallway, which is almost completely dark, and the hulk reaches around us to flip a light switch. The bulb goes on, then instantly pops and explodes. I yelp as thin slivers of glass rain down on us. The hulk mutters a curse, jumping out of the way. Lucien steps backward, and a shadow falls across his face. It's the light coming in from the corridor we just left. I look at him in that half-light, and something dark unfurls inside me. An old thing. A fear. A rage. And I find I can't look away.

He grins that wicked, demonic grin I remember from when I was little, and he'd pretend to want to play with me only to hurt me. It's the same face he wore then.

He twists my arm, and that darkness expands into every cell of my body, and all at once, it's like that heavy, once-impenetrable lid is opened. My knees buckle under the weight of images, thoughts, feelings and screams as it all comes back to me.

Lucien dragging me into that house. Down those stairs.

Lucien locking my wrists in those chains.

Lucien standing back when the two men walk into that room, lighting a cigarette, another thing my father hated that he did, and dropping bills on the floor. Fifteen-hundred dollars.

And finally, Lucien walking away, leaving me with those men, that grinning demon's face the last thing I saw before I saw their faces. Felt their hands.

Sweat drenches me. I look at him, my half brother, a man who hates me, who has always hated me so much more than I ever even knew. And I remember.

"It was you," I say in a whisper.

The hulk shoves us forward, and we move, my eyes locked on the side of Lucien's face as he half drags me. Does he hear me? Does he understand that I know? I know what he did.

"In," the hulk says, pushing the heavy metal door open.

"It was you," I say, louder this time. I dig my heels in when he tries to pull me through the door. "You." He looks at me, eyes flat again, dead again, and I'm not sure if he doesn't understand or if this is him understanding. This is him feeling no remorse. Nothing at all. "You gave me to them. You did that."

Lucien cocks his head to the side, lifting one corner of his mouth.

My rage burns hot, and I reach for the pistol in the holster at the hulk's hip. He's faster than me, though, and stronger and almost breaks my hand. He shoves me away so hard I hit the wall, my head bouncing off it, and I go down. Stars dance before my eyes, and I'm stunned.

I know what happened to me now. I understand the nightmares.

And I know it was him.

I force my eyes to focus on the shoes in front of me. I look up at Lucien. But it's not a man I see. It's a monster.

He reaches down casually to grab my arm and haul me to my feet.

"It was also me who told them not to kill you. Thought that was a mistake, but you're going to get me out of a mess now, so I guess the old saying is true. Everything happens for a reason."

He tugs me painfully across the threshold, and the metal door clangs shut behind us. I drag my gaze from my demon brother and look around the room and understand what he's saying. What I'm going to get him out of.

Because this room is full of men. Dangerous men. Soldiers. They go quiet, and all eyes turn to us. To me.

I try to get free, but Lucien's hold is like a vise. I scan the sea of faces and immediately see the one in charge. There's an air about him. He takes a step toward us and looks at my brother with irritation, but when his eyes land on me, he stops short. His expression changes, face morphing into something completely other.

And my own heart stops because I know who he is. I know exactly who he is.

## 27

## AMADEO

My phone rings shortly after we drive out of the garage in one of Sonny's cars.

"I just had a call," he says, sounding anxious. "There's activity in an abandoned school building about an hour north of Naples. I'm sending the address. Dmitri Anders is supposedly there. Authorities are getting ready to pick him up."

"Why would we care about Dmitri Anders?" I ask.

"Those photos you sent of the mystery man with Leah Russo? The tattoos identify him as being that man."

"Vittoria's mother was having an affair with Dmitri Anders? The same man we're talking about having a financial link to Lucien Russo?" Bastian asks.

"One and the same."

I look at Bastian, who appears as confused as me.

"On the school, Lucien Russo called in the tip," Bruno adds. "Made some sort of arrangement is what my contact is telling me. So he's likely there. He and Sonny may have been working together. They have before. And if he had those photos of Leah and Anders, he could be using Vittoria to save his own neck. Anders will want payment for the lost men."

"And Vittoria will be that payment," I say.

"That's insane. The man had an affair with her mother. Using Vittoria is... sick."

"He's desperate," I say.

"And we don't know anything about Dmitri Anders or his relationship with Leah. Not to mention his morals or ethics."

"Calling the authorities is his backup plan," I say, understanding. It's all that makes sense. "He's hoping they'll pick Anders up in case Anders doesn't accept the payment."

"Could be," Bruno says.

"Could he be Emma's father?" Bastian asks.

"Haven't had a chance to do more than identify the tattoos," Bruno says.

"How far are we from the school?" I ask as Bastian enters the address of the building into the GPS.

"You're about an hour out. If you backtrack about four miles, I can get the chopper out there," Bruno says, tracking our location. "It'll be faster than driving. There's a clearing where he can land. You'll see it from the road."

We're on a long stretch of road, and although I see the headlights of a car coming toward us, I hit the brakes and jerk the steering wheel. Bastian curses, grabbing the handhold as the car skids, bouncing off the road before I right it and head back the way we came. Because this is our only big lead.

"On our way," Bastian says. "If my brother doesn't kill us first."

"I'll call you as I learn more," Bruno says. "If the authorities are there, Amadeo, you can't be, understand?"

"If Vittoria is there, I'm getting her out. Fuck the authorities. Get men out there. Men we trust."

"It'll take time."

"Do it." I disconnect the call and drive as fast as the car will go to the clearing. The chopper comes into view as we pull off the road. I stop the car, leaving the keys in the ignition when Bastian and I climb out. The chopper touches down, and we're on board in record time and in the air in the next minute. Two of our men are already on board and one unzips the duffel bag to display an array of firepower. I have a feeling we won't be getting even the smallest pistol into that building if Dmitri Anders is there. He and his men will be armed, and it's not like we can make a quiet entrance with the chopper.

Bastian points out the window to the road as, in the distance, the headlights of a row of black SUVs with official markings makes its way to our destination. They'll be slower than us. We'll have time to get Vittoria out, if she's there.

*If.*

I don't like the desperation I feel at the word. The

anxiety. And a glance at Bastian tells me he's just as anxious as me.

We watch out the window, the lights of that procession disappearing into the night. What feels like an eternity later, a lone building comes into view. It looks like it's been abandoned for a very long time. Outside, three SUVs are parked along with one sedan. Two men standing sentry look up at us, readying their weapons as the chopper lands some distance away.

"Wait here," I tell the pilot. "If you see Vittoria, pick her up. Get her out of here and get in touch with Bruno for instructions. Do not wait for us, understand?"

He nods.

I turn to Bastian. "Ready?"

"I've been ready for fifteen years."

We climb out, ducking our heads and sticking our arms in the air so the soldiers don't shoot before we even get there. The chopper's propellors stir up a dust storm, and once we clear it, we walk slowly toward the building, very aware of the machine guns pointing directly at us.

Once we're near enough that they can hear us, we stop. "Tell Dmitri there's a convoy coming for him. They're about twenty minutes out at most. We came to warn him."

The one looks at the other, who steps toward. "Who the fuck are you?"

"Amadeo Caballero. This is my brother, Bastian. He'll know our names. Tell him we're here for my wife.

We'll take him with us if he wants, but we won't be leaving without her."

He turns to his companion, who is on the radio with someone. Whoever was on the radio must have heard our conversation because a moment later, two huge men come to the door and look us over.

"Search them," one says.

Bastian and I stand still and let them take our pistols. We're then escorted inside one man ahead of us, the other behind. I look into each of the rooms we pass, but the building is empty.

Just as we reach the door at the end of the corridor, I hear a scream, a sound like nothing I've heard before.

Vittoria.

I thrust the door open, slamming it against the wall, and Bastian and I charge inside, the sound of a fury so hot it carries over that of weapons being drawn, armed, and what I see, fuck. What I see stops us both dead.

## 28

## VITTORIA

I stare into the ice-blue eyes of my mother's lover, and he stares right back into mine. He walks toward me, stands a few inches from me, and I look down at his arm, at the ink that I recognize, knowing these were the arms my mother took comfort in.

His gaze moves to my brother's hand. Lucien is still holding on to me. He cocks his head then looks at Lucien.

"Take your hand off her."

"She's payment," Lucien says, thrusting me toward the tattooed man as I study him. This stranger who knew my mother so intimately. The man with whom she looked happy.

"Is she?" he asks, dragging his gaze to my face once more, searching it again before returning his full attention to Lucien. "What are you playing at, boy?" he asks, closing his calloused, scarred hand over Lucien's wrist and removing it from my arm.

I rub the spot he held me and step away from them both. Just one step. I just need a little space.

"Not playing, Dmitri. She's payment for the lost soldiers. Thought you'd want that, considering."

Dmitri. I have no idea who he is. Never heard my mother utter his name. Dmitri's eyes search my face again as if searching for something. Or more likely, someone, I guess. How could she have been with someone like this? He seems dangerous and cold. Rough. My father was elegant. Subtle. Although was he any less dangerous? Any less rough? What drove my mother into the arms of a stranger?

But one thing at a time. Dmitri will have to wait. I turn back to Lucien, remembering it all, the basement, those men. It's that nightmare that comes like clockwork in the weeks leading up to my birthday except it's the real version. The part that happened. It's the memory Tilbury tried to fucking electrocute out of my brain. But things didn't go exactly right, I guess. He erased a full year, and now it's come rushing back.

My dad came for me. I remember that, too. He was too late, though. They'd already broken me. And I'd killed them for it.

I look down at my bruised, scratched hands. My bloody hands.

I can see Dad's face in my mind's eye as clear as day. His eyes when he saw me with the gun still in my hand. All that blood on me. All that blood staining every surface. I think seeing that broke him a little too.

He carried me out of there. And then came the incident with the bleach and then Dr. Tilbury.

"Considering," Dmitri says, calling me back into the present. He takes a half step away, one corner of his mouth curved upward but not in any way close to a smile. He's thinking. Calculating. "It was you, wasn't it? You were the one who blackmailed her with those photos."

My mouth falls open. What? Lucien blackmailed my mother?

"What did you do?" I start, making a move toward Lucien. Dmitri effortlessly catches me and keeps me tight to his side, one arm wrapped around me to trap me against him. He barely looks at me. Just studies Lucien closely like he's putting a puzzle together as I struggle to remove the steel bar that is his arm.

"I tried to get you your daughter, but Sonny's men screwed that up. You can trade Vittoria for the kid."

A trade? For Emma? What the hell is he talking about? I stop struggling, confused. I turn to look at Dmitri's face. His ice-blue eyes.

Dmitri grins, passing me off to one of his men, and I watch as he steps right up to Lucien.

"The little girl isn't mine. But I think you already know that."

I watch, dumbstruck as Dmitri walks a menacing circle around Lucien, then comes to stand in front of him.

"I think I understand things now."

Lucien looks back at me, then around at all the

men. He miscalculated. And he knows it. He nervously checks his watch.

Dmitri takes him by the back of the neck and forces him to look up at him. "You have somewhere to be, boy?"

"The kid's yours. I swear."

"Impossible. *Medically* impossible."

It takes a moment for the color to bleed from Lucien's face, and I get a feeling Dmitri's calm tone is a warning of the rage to come rather than anything else.

"She was going to come away with me. Did you know that?" He turns to me. "But she wouldn't leave you behind. That's why I let her stay in that house, knowing what I knew." He turns back to Lucien. "But that day, she'd come to leave me." He shakes his head. "I demanded to know if it was that bastard husband, if he'd raped her, because I was going to kill him. I was halfway out the door to kill that motherfucker like I should have done when I saw the first bruise. But she stopped me. She told me she was leaving me. She had to, or he'd take her children from her when he found out about us. She showed me a photo and told me there were more. So many more. And if she didn't walk away, her husband would see them, and she knew he'd take away the thing she loved most."

Tears fall for my mother. I sob for her. For the sadness of her life. For the loss of her.

"You look like her. So much like her. You even cry like her," he says to me. "I don't think I'll ever forget that sound of her sobbing. She had no choice, she said, and I understood." He releases Lucien and looks at me. "I loved her enough to understand why she was choosing her children over us."

I feel a kinship with this stranger whose eyes shine with emotion at the memory of my mother. He loved her.

"My mistake." His voice is so hard, the shift so unexpected, that it chills me. He gives Lucien his full attention. "My mistake was that I let her go. I left her alone and unprotected in a house with the likes of you. Of your father. And you killed her."

Lucien swallows hard and shakes his head. "That wasn't me. That was Dad."

"Yeah?" Dmitri asks, grabbing him by the hair on the back of his head and tugging his head backward. "Explain."

"He had the mechanic rig the brakes. Arranged for a car chase. He couldn't stand looking at her after he found out the truth."

"And how did he find it out? The photos should have been destroyed. It's why she did it. Why she slept with you."

"What?" I hear myself ask. My brain rattles inside my head, and it feels like the world drops out from under my feet. "What did you do?" I ask in a voice I don't recognize. "What did you do?" I scream. Finding a strength I didn't know I had, I break away from the man who has me. I hurl myself at Lucien, wrapping my legs around him and digging my nails into his skin as he stumbles backward. He and I go down as one, my scream deafening.

A door slams open somewhere behind me. I hear the commotion of weapons being drawn. And I feel hands on me trying to pry me off as a rage I've never felt before gives me the strength to plunge my fingers into Lucien's eye sockets. He screams and screams like he made me scream. And I know I'm not going to stop. I'm going to kill him with my bare hands. I'm going to dig out his eyes and then his heart and crush it with my bare hands and make him pay for what he did. For everything he did.

## 29

## VITTORIA

"What did you do to her? What did you do to my mother?"

Did he rape my mother? Impregnate her? Did he blackmail her into sleeping with him? Threaten to expose her affair to Dad who I know would take me away from her. Would have taken Emma away if only to hurt her.

Emma.

Oh God, Emma. She's Lucien's?

Arms close around me, gentler than I'd expect. Lucien lies whimpering, and I slap wet hands against his chest as the energy drains from me.

"What did you do?" I ask again, this time my voice quieter.

"Dandelion."

"What did you do to her? To me?"

Gentle hands haul me up. They turn me around and hold me tight, and I sob into Amadeo's chest. I sob.

And when Bastian's hand comes to the back of my head, I shift into his arms and hold them both tight. I sob for all of it, all the loss. The senseless loss. My mother, myself, Emma, our father.

I need to know one more thing. Did he kill Dad too? Will I ever know? I try to stop sobbing long enough to get air in. To ask the question. But the tears won't stop.

"Get her out of here," Amadeo says, handing me off to Bastian.

"Wait," I cry out.

I wipe my eyes with the backs of my hands. They're covered in blood and gunk, and Bastian holds me as I turn to look at my brother one final time. Because he won't walk out of here today. Today, he'll pay for what he did. And it's not only me he owes.

I look down at Lucien. His face is unrecognizable. His eye sockets are blood, just blood, and he's sobbing. I look at Dmitri, who is watching me.

"Give me your gun," I say to him.

"Vittoria," Amadeo says.

"Give it to me!"

"You don't want any more of his blood on your hands," Dmitri says. "You don't want his soul linked to yours." I open my mouth to speak, but he goes first, and what he says silences me. "Your mother wouldn't want that, Vittoria."

My mother. He's the reason she's gone. Lucien is the reason.

I close my eyes and turn my face into Bastian's

chest, and he just holds me tight because Dmitri is right. And to know that he knew my mother so intimately is a strange, bitter comfort.

"How far out is the convoy?" Dmitri asks.

"Ten minutes if you're lucky," Amadeo says.

"Chopper?"

"Outside. Give me your gun."

Dmitri hands him his gun.

Amadeo nods. "Go. Bastian, take her."

"Amadeo, you can't be the one to stay," Bastian says.

Amadeo looks at me, then at his brother. "This ends today. Here and now. Get her out of here."

"They'll take you in—"

"She needs you. Get her out."

Bastian is clearly not happy about this, but he looks down at me, wraps an arm around me, and we walk out. The three of us along with two of Dmitri's men board the chopper, the others leaving with the SUVs. And I imagine I hear the sound of the gun being fired although I know that's impossible with the noise of the blades. But I know it's over now. It's finally over.

## 30

## AMADEO

"Who's there? Who the fuck is there?" Lucien asks, his voice frantic as he tries to scramble to a seat.

I put my foot against his chest to stop him. He freezes. I check Dmitri's gun, and I'm happy to find a full round of bullets. I only wish I had more time.

Lucien tries to pull away when I crouch down. "Who the fuck is it?" he screams.

"It's Amadeo Del Campo. Hannah's big brother," I tell him. No need to keep him in the dark. Although I guess he'll live the remaining few minutes of his life in the dark. "You look disgusting, you know that?"

"What do you want?"

"What do you think I want?" I ask as I hear the screech of the first of the SUVs of the convoy arriving.

"They're here! They're here, you fucking bastard!"

"I would watch what you call me right about now,"

I say, putting the barrel of the pistol to where his tiny cock is and pulling the trigger.

Lucien screams, and it's fucking music to my ears.

"That was for Hannah. This next one is for my dad," I say, hearing footsteps charging into the building. I put the barrel on his right knee and pull the trigger, then bring it to his left knee as Lucien sobs and screams. "This will be for my mom." I blow out his other knee. By now, given the state he's in, he should be begging for death.

"Please. Please. Fuck. Please."

"I'm short on time, so I'm going to have to make the last one good. It'll be for the rest of us. Vittoria. Her mother. My brother. Me. Even little Emma." I point at his stomach, which will be the most painful and slowest way for him to go. I pull the trigger just as the door is knocked down. Men descend upon me, throwing me facedown to the ground, kicking the gun from my hand before slapping handcuffs on my wrists and hauling me to my feet.

"Well, well," my old enemy, Chief Inspector Greco says. "Mr. Caballero."

"Chief Greco, good to see you, as always."

Greco signals to one of his men who delivers a punch to my gut that would have me doubling over if it wasn't for the two holding me upright.

"It's never good to see you. What's this?" He looks down at Lucien, who is bleeding out and begging for help. "What a mess," he says. "That's two you've killed today, is that right?"

Lucien stills. "No! No! You said… I called it in! You… Help me! Fucking help me!"

"Busy day, or is that normal?" Greco asks me calmly.

I grin. "Slow, actually."

"Where's the Russian?"

"Who?"

He shakes his head, and I smile. It's a good day. "I'll see you in prison," he says close to my ear. "I have good friends there."

"I look forward to it. I'm sure we'll have a lot to discuss. Starting with those cash deposits into your wife's account," I whisper the last part.

That wipes anything resembling satisfaction off his face, and he gestures to the cops to take me away.

## 31

## BASTIAN

"You're a mess, Dandelion. Remind me not to fuck with you."

Vittoria sits in the tub looking straight ahead as I scrub blood and dirt off her. I take each of her fingers and clean the gunk of Lucien's eyes and skin out from under her broken nails. I drain the tub once, twice, three times and refill it and all the while she sits there staring straight at nothing, almost catatonic.

Someone brings a steaming mug of tea. I thank them and set it aside to cool a little while I wash her hair then put conditioner in it to comb it through, taking my time. I like doing it. She finally closes her eyes and lets her head drop back. I watch her face, soft and relaxed, and I think about all the shit she's been through. The things that have been done to her. And I make a vow at that moment. I will not allow anyone to harm her again. I will never let anything happen to our Dandelion ever again.

I rinse the conditioner out of her hair, then crouch down beside the tub. "Vittoria, drink this." She doesn't stir. I bring the cup of tea to her lips. "Dandelion."

She turns to me, finally looks at me with soft, yielding eyes. They're so expressive, those eyes.

"You're beautiful, you know that?" She blinks, giving me the smallest smile. I brush a strand of wet hair back from her face. "Drink this."

I hold it to her mouth, and she takes a sip, then another, then brings handfuls of water to her face and rubs her eyes. I watch her, wondering if she's crying again. I don't even think it's conscious, that crying. Just years' worth of locked up emotion.

"Come on. You're going to get cold," I say, unplugging the drain and getting an oversized towel to wrap her in. She stands, water falling off her too-thin body. The stress of it all, I imagine. She lets me wrap her in the towel, and when I lift her out of the tub, she puts her arms around my neck and watches me in that way she has as I carry her into the bedroom. It's a little unsettling, I admit, but this is her. This is Dandelion. A little weird. Damaged. But ours.

*Ours.*

At that, my mind wanders to Amadeo. I don't know where they've taken him.

Vittoria touches my face, calling me back to her. I muster a smile and set her down, then begin to dry her. She lets me, and I like it. I like taking care of her. It's strange. I've never felt this way for any other woman before.

"Emma?" she asks once she's dry.

"She's safe. She was hiding behind all those stuffed animals."

"Good."

"She called for help, Vittoria. That's how I found her."

Her forehead furrows. "She spoke?"

I nod. "In whispers but yes, she's talking. I think she's trying to get used to the sound of her own voice."

Vittoria's mouth stretches into a smile, but it's only momentary as that line between her eyebrows deepens, and she begins to cry quiet tears.

"It was him," she says. "It was all him. All the damage he did. All the people he hurt…"

I hug her to me, taking her weight when she leans into me, holding her tight as her body is wracked by her tears.

"He's gone now, Vittoria. It's over. He's dead."

"Emma is his."

I take her face in my hands, push her hair back, and make her look at me.

"Emma is your mother's. Period."

"She's not like him. She's nothing like him," she says, still crying. "She's—

"She's not, Dandelion. I know that. She's like you," I say, and this seems to calm her. "She's a sweet kid. Smart too. We do need to get her some new shoes, though. Hers are ratty and, if I'm being honest, a little smelly." I make a face that has the desired effect of making her almost smile.

"Mom gave them to her for her birthday last year. She's worn them every day since the accident." She pauses at the word accident because it wasn't that. It was murder. "Where is she?"

"In Sicily with our mother."

"I didn't even ask. Your mom is okay?"

I nod.

"I'm glad. But where's Hyacinth?"

I take a beat too long, and she knows the answer before I even have to speak. Her eyes fill with fresh tears. I pull her to me, and she lets me hold her for a long time before drawing back.

"Have you heard from Amadeo?" she asks.

"He'll be here soon." I'm not actually sure about that, but Bruno found Sonny's file on Greco and plenty of other dirty cops, politicians, and judges and has been contacting the appropriate people. He doesn't know where they took my brother, either. But I'm not telling Vittoria that.

"But he's not hurt?"

"He's strong, Dandelion. Like you," I answer, not really answering.

Her eyes lose focus momentarily. "My dad told me that, you know. When he found me there with their bodies." She shakes her head as if to dislodge the image. "He told me what doesn't kill you makes you stronger. He left out the part about how when you break like that, you're never quite fixed. Fixable."

"He was right. And you don't need to be fixed. That damage is a part of you. A part of what makes you a survivor," I say, needing time to get my thoughts about Geno Russo straight, and also in some way understanding I'm saying this as much about myself as her. "They're long dead. And you're still standing." She looks down, not convinced. I tilt her head up. "Like a fucking dandelion. Dandelions survive when everything else dies. They'll sprout up out of a fucking crack in the pavement. It kind of fits, you have to say."

"Is that an attempt at a compliment?" she asks, a little of her humor coming back.

I shrug a shoulder. "Just trying to keep you out of your head. What's happened, what you learned and remembered... it's a lot. You're going to need time to process. But you can't disappear into your head alone. I don't think that's good for you."

She shivers and hugs the towel to herself.

"Let's get you dressed."

"Do you know where he is, though? Amadeo?"

I shake my head. If I did, I'd be there. And I'm worried. Because he's alone and they can hurt us when we're divided. I know that well enough.

"I want to wait for him."

I nod, then walk her into the closet to get her dressed in a pair of leggings and a comfortable, oversized sweater. She leads the way downstairs and curls up on the sofa, facing the front door. I bring the whiskey and pour some for each of us, but neither of us drinks as we keep vigil.

## 32

## VITTORIA

Bastian and I sit side by side in the living room and wait. Neither of us touches the whiskey. He's worried. I can see it. And he doesn't want to let on.

It's almost over. This nightmare at least finished. I don't know that any of us feel better for it. I don't. Does Bastian feel some satisfaction at the death of my brother? Because he is dead. I have no doubt of that. Do I for tearing out his eyes?

I look down at my hands, turning them over. I know why I did that after the dreams now. I was searching for blood. I couldn't get it off at first even when I scrubbed the skin raw with bleach.

But Bastian has cleaned them well and with such care. The only evidence of the violence my hands did is in the broken, jagged fingernails.

Lucien paid those men to keep me prisoner. To hurt me. He hated me so much he delivered me to them. He hated my mother as much. But I think he also always wanted her. He blackmailed her into leaving her lover. Did he rape her? Or did he blackmail her into sleeping with him? Either way, it's rape. She didn't want him. But the result is Emma, and my mother adored Emma. She took so much care with her. She didn't hate her as the product of that sort of coupling.

Then there is Dmitri Anders. He loved my mother. I could see that in his eyes. If he'd stayed with her, if he'd made her stay, would she be here today?

At that, my mind wanders to my father. Lucien accused him of my mother's murder, but can I trust anything he says? They're all dead now, so I may never know the truth. Was my father truly capable of violence like that? He hated Emma. I saw that for myself. I saw how ugly he could be to her.

"Get out of your head, Dandelion," Bastian says, taking one of my hands and weaving his fingers with mine.

I look over at him. My dragon. One of two. Emma trusts him. I trust him. I trust them both. What will we do now that it's over? Now that there truly is nothing more I can give them? Will they let us go? Do I want them to?

He squeezes that hand, and I look down at his lap, at our hands together. My right in his left. And I lay my head on his shoulder and fit myself into him.

Hours must pass because the sun has broken the horizon, turning the sky a deep orange before we hear the sound of tires crunching gravel. Keeping my hand in his, Bastian is on his feet, and I am on mine. My heart is in my stomach, and when the door opens, and Amadeo walks in looking like he's walked through hell, I feel a release so overwhelming, so emotionally charged, I cry out as fresh warm tears of relief stream down my face. I exhale. I finally exhale. And when my knees buckle with the emotion of it all, I know I'm only upright because Bastian is holding me.

"You look like shit," Bastian says, releasing me to hug his brother.

"Thanks," Amadeo says, hugging him back. They pat each other on the back the way men do, and when they pull away, Amadeo's eyes land on me. He glances at Bastian, and they share some silent exchange before Amadeo steps toward me. I think he must be able to hear my heartbeat because it's pounding so hard it's all I can hear.

"Dandelion," he says. I missed his voice. The assurance of it. The strength of it.

I look up into his steel-colored eyes that I don't find cold anymore. And I do something that surprises me maybe more than it surprises either of them. I pour myself into his arms and hug him hard while my body is wracked by a wave of relief and something else. Something I never thought I'd feel for these men. My captors. My dragons. My lovers.

In my periphery I see Bastian. He turns away as if unable to look at this display, but before he can walk away, I reach out to take his hand and draw him to me.

And as we stand there, all three of us, Amadeo beaten, bruised, and splattered with what I know is Lucien's blood, Bastian, disheveled from the events of the day, from looking after me so carefully that he neglected himself completely, and me, the daughter of their enemy. The sister. A Russo. And as we stand in our small circle, I know one thing more surely than I've ever known anything in my life. We were fated, the three of us, from a very young age and from before the events that took place in that small kitchen on that terrible day, to come to this place. This moment in time. We were always meant to end up right here. Together.

Amadeo told me once when you kill a man, their soul is bound to yours for eternity. I don't believe that, though. I think you can only be bound to those you love. To those who your heart swells and drops for.

I reach up to first kiss Amadeo and then Bastian. I weave my fingers with theirs and lead them up the stairs to my bedroom. The three of us. And as they wipe the tears that fall while they make love to me and I too them, I know that we belong to each other. The three of us, we have always belonged to each other.

## 33

## AMADEO

I watch Dandelion sleep. She is spent and it's not just the lovemaking. It's the hours before, the days, the months, the years. And now she's here. In our house. In our beds. Ours.

Bastian steps out of the bathroom freshly showered. He, too, looks at her, with her wild blond hair fanned out over the pillow, her face so soft in sleep. Lips still swollen from our kisses.

"I'm going to get dressed," Bastian says. "Meet out back?"

I nod and see the moment he takes before walking out of that room. We're thinking the same thing, my brother and me. Because the reason for this, it's over. Finished. Lucien Russo is dead. Geno Russo was already dead. Russo Properties & Holdings itself hardly seems to matter. The erasure of the Russo name from the face of the earth is a fading memory. Because what matters is the woman sleeping on the bed. Because she has changed everything.

Ten minutes later Bastian walks out onto the back patio where I'm seated looking out over the sea at the clear, beautiful morning. No clouds in the distance. No storms on the horizon.

"What happened?" Bastian asks as he takes a seat.

I pour him a mug of coffee from the carafe on the table.

"Greco got a minute to flex his muscle." Greco ordered my beating, then denied having done so. Fucking coward. "I'll repay him in kind in my own time."

"Bruno came through?"

"Yeah. Uncle Sonny was very good at one thing. He kept very precise records and had an excellent surveillance system in place."

Bastian grins. "Always covered his ass, the prick."

"Thanks to Sonny we won't have any trouble with the authorities going forward."

"Good. Mom and Emma are good. Just talked to Stefan."

"Thanks for doing that. Bruno said the cleaners will be done with the Ravello house in a few days. What do you think? Keep it? Go back?"

"I think it'll be hard for Mom and Emma," he says.

"Emma."

He looks out to the sea, jaw tight, because here it is. The thing we are here to discuss. Dandelion.

After a long minute he turns to me.

"I know the right thing to do. But what I want to do is very different," he says.

I drink a sip of steaming coffee and study my brother. He wants to keep Vittoria. I understand. I feel the same way.

"It has to be up to her, brother," I say, turning to watch the soft waves of a calm sea.

"Like I said, I know the right thing."

"Bruno is getting paperwork ready for me to remove my hold on her finances."

Bastian nods. "Good."

We fall silent, each of us lost in our thoughts.

In a way, I wish Tilbury's treatment had been more thorough. That she wouldn't ever remember that year of her life. But she has, and she'll need to process. I have no doubt she can and will. If not for herself, then for Emma.

The patio door opens, and I turn, expecting one of the staff, but am surprised to find Vittoria walking toward us. She's barefoot, wearing one of my T-shirts, her hair loose and wild down her back.

She's fucking beautiful to watch. Like something not quite of this earth. Not quite human. Or maybe too human. She is self-assured. She knows she is damaged, but she doesn't hide it or try to be something else. She is our Dandelion, a little strange, a little lonely maybe, a lot sad, but ours.

"Coffee?" I ask as she comes to settle on the grass at our feet.

She shakes her head and looks over her shoulder at

the view. "It's beautiful here."

I'm not sure my brother or I can drag our eyes from her. "Emma's on her way," I tell her. They should be landing any minute now.

"Already?" She seems surprised.

I nod.

"Really?"

"Really."

She smiles, but then her eyes darken. "Lucien," she says.

"He's dead."

"Did he suffer?"

"He suffered."

"Good." She picks at the grass before turning her gaze to mine. "I want to ask you something," she says, clearly anxious.

"What is it?"

She worries her lip with her teeth and doesn't speak until I see a drop of crimson from where she bites through skin. "I want to bury my father properly."

"Dandelion—"

She puts up a hand to stop me. "He made a lot of poor choices. A lot." Bastian snorts and she gives him a look but turns back to me. "But when it came to me, I think he was trying."

Bastian glances at me and I at him. She shifts her attention to the grass again.

"He was afraid of my grandfather. My grandfather thought him weak. And I think ultimately, he was afraid of Lucien," she finally adds then turns her gaze up to us. "What he did was wrong. He shouldn't have let Lucien hurt your sister. He should have done more then. But he was punished through me."

"Dandelion," Bastian starts when her eyes fill with tears.

She shakes her head. "You don't have to forgive him. I'm not asking that. But he was my father, and he was capable of love, and I think he regretted a lot of things." Her forehead furrows and she looks at each of us in turn. She's not done yet, I think, she's just trying to muster her courage to say what she needs to say. "He behaved like a coward and so many of us paid the price for that cowardice. You have every right to hate him. I know that and I know I'm asking a lot, but I want to rebury him. Do it properly. Give him some peace in death because I don't think he had any in life."

Bastian stands, takes a deep breath in and exhales slowly. She stands too, captures his hands in hers when she thinks he's going to walk away.

"Stay," she says. "Please."

"You should get dressed. You'll want to be ready when Emma gets here," he tells her.

"Please," she pleads, looking first up at him, then at me.

My cell phone buzzes with a text and get to my feet to dig it out of my pocket. Saved by the text. "Go get dressed, Vittoria. They're in the car on their way."

"But my father—"

"Later," I say after a glance at my brother. "Get ready for Emma. We'll talk later."

## 34

## VITTORIA

My reunion with Emma is more than I could have asked for and better than I imagined it could be. She walks toward the house cautiously at first, with her little pink schoolbag on her back, holding her stuffed pig in one hand and the other tucked safely into Nora's. But the instant she sees me when I throw the door open, she stops, her eyes growing huge with surprise, then happiness. She drops Nora's hand and charges toward me, hurling herself into my arms and nearly toppling me.

"Emma! Oh, Emma!" I cry into her hair, smelling a vanilla scented shampoo I don't recognize, hugging her tiny body to mine as she hugs me with all her force for so long, it brings tears to my eyes to think of what this child, this five-year-old child has gone through, has seen. The evil she knows exists in the world she lives in.

I draw back, wiping my eyes and nose and look at her face, pushing her hair away. I look into her eyes and I'm so happy that I don't see Lucien in them. I see nothing of him. Only Emma, my sweet little sister. And I hug her again, lifting her with me as I stand.

Nora joins us having picked up Emma's discarded backpack. She smiles kindly.

"She's such a good girl," she says to me as she rubs Emma's back. "Like Hannah was. So good."

I look at the older woman for a moment and see her sadness. And I understand the brothers' hesitation to grant me my wish to rebury my father. He destroyed their lives. Separate from what Lucien did, my father was just as guilty to cover it up, to try to bury it. He could have stopped it, but he chose a different path and his choices caused too much harm.

I reach one arm to Nora and pull her into our hug too and she so easily hugs me back. I think maybe, just maybe, we can start to heal now. All of us. I don't think the damage will ever be repaired wholly. There will always be cracks. But Bastian is right. Those cracks make us strong and they can be beautiful in their own way.

"Vittoria," I hear in my ear and blink away my tears because it's Emma. It's Emma's sweet little voice that I haven't heard in too long. So long that I'd forgotten it.

I draw back and set her down, crouching to be at eye level.

"Yes, sweetheart?" I ask, trying not to cry.

"Vittoria," she says again. Then points behind me. "Bastian. Amadeo." Then to Nora. "Nana."

Nana.

I don't correct her.

"You, little one, need to learn to put your shoes on the right feet," Bastian says, coming to sweep her up. Amadeo ruffles her hair, and I watch them with her. My two dragons are so sweet to this child as Bastian slides one shoe off and makes a point of sniffing it, then pretending to pass out, only to have her giggling. The sound of her laughter grows as he tickles her and does it again with her other shoe, and it's the most wonderful thing.

"Happy?" Amadeo asks, startling me. I didn't realize he'd come to stand right behind me. He's holding his mother's hand in one of his and sets the other against my lower back.

I turn my face up to his, kiss his cheek. "Happy," I say.

---

WE SPEND THE WHOLE DAY SWIMMING IN THE POOL, THEN playing on the beach, then back to the pool until I put an exhausted Emma to bed at a little before eight at night. We've had dinner, and the brothers are upstairs with their mother. She's exhausted, too, and I didn't realize that the man and woman traveling with them were a doctor and nurse.

They've asked me to meet them in the study so I'm

watching the moon in the distance trying to decide if the morning is more beautiful or the night.

"Dandelion," Bastian says, entering first. His mood is heavy, and I wonder if it's because of his mother. If she's unwell.

Amadeo follows him looking tired.

"Is she okay?" I ask as they close the door.

"She'll have to be. Physically, she's fine, but she saw it happen." When I wait for more, he reluctantly adds, "Francesca and Hyacinth."

I cover my mouth. "Oh, God."

"Having Emma is helping her immensely," Bastian says.

"And Emma having her is helping Emma too, I think. When I came back after the will reading, you should have seen her. They'd made me a birthday cake, and Emma just looked relaxed and happy and not afraid for the first time in so long."

Amadeo comes to me, rubs my back and hugs me. "She'll get that back. She's young and strong and she has you, Vittoria."

Just me? I want to ask but don't.

"What will you do now?" I ask, using the heels of my hands to wipe the stray tears. "Ravello, I mean. Will you keep it?"

"Not sure. I think it might be too much for Mom."

"And Emma," I say, searching his eyes.

He searches mine too.

I open my mouth to say what I need to say, but before I can get a word out, there's a knock on the door, and Bruno enters carrying a briefcase. He looks at all three of us but when he takes Amadeo in is when his smile broadens.

"Evening everyone," he says, going to Amadeo. "Good to see you in one piece, my friend." He hugs Amadeo and Amadeo hugs him back.

"It's good to be in one piece," Amadeo says. "I owe that to you."

Bruno brushes that off and turns to us. "Bastian, Vittoria," he says, setting his briefcase down on the desk and opening it. "Everyone is well?"

I nod as Bastian says something I don't hear because I'm watching him unpack a folder and arrange official-looking papers.

Once he's done, he closes his briefcase and sets it aside.

"I have everything here ready to sign," he says with a glance at me but directing his words to Amadeo.

I look at the brothers. "What are we signing?"

Amadeo steps forward while Bastian remains where he is, watching as he sips whiskey.

"Since Brady no longer works for Russo Properties & Holdings, Bruno took over temporarily just to do what needed to be done," Amadeo explains.

I stare up at him, glancing at Bastian for a clue but getting nothing.

Amadeo touches my cheek to call my attention to himself. His gaze is intent on me like he's still searching for whatever it was he was looking for before Bruno entered.

"I'm signing it all back to you, Vittoria."

"What?"

He smiles, takes the pen from Bruno and, before answering, signs where the older man tells him to sign. He then turns to me. "I no longer have control of your shares or your finances. I have no stake in Russo Properties & Holdings."

"I... don't understand."

"It's back to you." He holds the pen out to me. "As it should be."

I take the pen, numb, and let him guide me toward the desk where Bruno points out where I should sign then explains that Lucien's shares also revert to me since his death. If I want to put anything aside for Emma, I can do that. He'll arrange it all.

I sign where he says for me to sign, glancing at Amadeo, at Bastian. He's still silent, and Amadeo has a strange look on his face. One I can't read. Regret? I'm not sure.

"That's everything," Bruno says, taking the pen from my hand and gathering up the paperwork. "I'll leave this one," he says to Amadeo who nods. I glance at the desk to the sealed envelope but wait to speak until Bruno is gone and the door is closed behind him.

"I don't understand," I say.

"What don't you understand? It was yours all along. Not mine. We got what we wanted." He gestures to Bastian, and my gaze follows his.

"Lucien dead, you mean," I say, my heart falling a little.

Amadeo just stares at me.

"What about us?" I look from one to the other. "Me?" I'm aware that the fingers of one hand inadvertently move to the wedding band on the other.

Amadeo's smile is forced now as he moves to pick up the envelope Bruno left. He breaks the seal and takes out the folded sheets of paper. He holds them out to me.

"What is it? Just tell me what it is," I hear myself snap as I take a step away as if the sheets of paper might burn me.

"Annulment."

I look at the sheets in his hand then up at him. "You can't annul the marriage. It's iron-clad. You made sure."

"I pulled some strings. You can be free, Dandelion. This can be erased."'

"Erased?" My eyes burn, my forehead furrows. "Like a year of my life was erased? What's a few more weeks?"

Amadeo steps toward me, concerned but also confused. I look at Bastian and see how the hand at his side is a fist.

"You want to erase it?" I ask, feeling my lip tremble. "Erase me?"

Amadeo looks at me gently. "No, sweetheart, I don't want to erase you. I don't want to erase us," Amadeo says.

"Then why?"

"It has to be your choice. You have to choose. I gave

you my word once. Freedom for you and Emma. It's yours. With the condition that it comes with our protection of course. At least until you…"

"Until I what?" I snatch the pages out of his hand and glance down at them, then toss them aside. "Until I what, Amadeo? Marry again? Have some other man to protect me because I need protecting?" I'm not sure if I'm more angry or hurt.

Amadeo's jaw tightens.

A low growl comes from Bastian. I give him one glance and see he's put his whiskey down. It's taking all he has to stay where he is and remain silent.

Amadeo steps toward me and takes my arms. "What do you want, Dandelion?"

"It doesn't matter. You don't want me."

"For fuck's sake," Bastian says. I'm not sure if he's talking to Amadeo or me when he comes to stand at my back, taking a fistful of hair and turning my head in his direction. "You think we don't want you?"

I look at his face, the pain I'd once glimpsed on it that had made it hard to look at him, I see it again, there, underneath everything. A constant. That's what damage does. It hovers. Ever present.

"I love you," I tell him. It comes out of nowhere. No, that's not right. It comes from my heart. "I love you, you fucking idiot!" I turn to Amadeo, slap my fists against his unmovable chest. "I fucking love you! You can't just erase me. Erase us. That's not how this works."

Amadeo laughs, takes me in his arms and pulls me

to him. "Oh, Dandelion, I was right about you, you know that?" he asks, not letting me get away when I struggle to. "You are absolutely insane."

"Fucking nuts," Bastian mutters at my back.

I look from one to the other.

"But I love you and if you choose to stay with us now, just know that we won't ever let you go," Amadeo says. "It just has to be your choice."

I turn to Bastian, surprised? Not sure. Happy? Yes.

"That goes for me too, Dandelion. I love you, sweetheart," he says, taking me from Amadeo as Amadeo releases me into Bastian's arms.

"But…"

"But nothing," Amadeo says. "We love you. We want you to stay. We want Emma to stay. I want my ring on your finger. I want you, Dandelion."

"Why even draw up those papers?"

"Because I gave you my word."

"I have one request," I hear myself saying, taking each of their hands.

"What's that?" Amadeo asks.

"Another wedding. Just us and Emma and your mom. Bruno too, if you want."

He looks confused, and I take Bastian's left hand. "I want to marry you both, and I know it's not legal, but fuck legal. I don't care about that. I just want to belong to you both. And I want you both to belong to me."

## EPILOGUE 1
BASTIAN

The three of us will say our vows on the beach. It's not a legal wedding. Nothing like that. On paper, she will be Amadeo's wife. But in reality, she will be ours. And the only people who matter are us so I'm with her when she says fuck legal.

Amadeo and I stand on the beach at the ass crack of dawn. I stifle a yawn as the sun breaks the horizon. Her idea. A new beginning. And sunrise was a better symbol of that to Vittoria.

I glance at my brother glad to see he looks as tired as I feel. Neither he nor I are morning people. But then the patio doors open, and Vittoria appears on the threshold holding Emma's hand in one of hers and a bouquet of dandelions in the other. If I know her, they went out to pick them this morning.

I clear my throat and straighten and my brother

does the same as we take in our bride wearing a simple white lace dress under which I see she's barefoot, her hair loose down her back and a crown of wildflowers bound together by dandelions in her hair.

Fuck.

She looks so beautiful wearing just some lip gloss and mascara and nothing else. She smiles as she makes her way toward us through the sand. I glance at Emma who takes careful steps along her big sister. She is wearing a smaller version of Vittoria's dress and has a matching crown in her hair.

Bruno accompanies my mother, and they follow Vittoria toward us, taking two of the three chairs. When Vittoria reaches us, Emma takes her bouquet and hands it off to my mother. Then, in a move she obviously practiced because she's so intent on getting it right that her tiny tongue is sticking out of her mouth, she takes Vittoria's hands and places one in mine and the other in Amadeo's.

Vittoria smiles down at her, and Emma takes her seat. As the sky turns orange, we make a promise to each other that we will be bound to one another. We will love and honor her and she us, and never be apart in our hearts for as long as we all shall live.

We exchange rings, simpler rings than the official wedding band she and Amadeo exchanged and designed especially for us. Platinum rings made to look like a single dandelion turned wish to wrap around each of our fingers. And as I place mine on the ring finger of Vittoria's right hand, I look into her glistening sapphire eyes and make a wish. For her. For her to be happy. And I vow that that is what I will strive to do for the rest of my days.

# EPILOGUE 2
## AMADEO

*Three Months Later*

For the first time since our grandfather's death, the Caballero family is united as one. Once the truth about Sonny putting the hit on his own son came out, most of those who had been loyal to him swore fealty to me. Those who didn't were dealt with.

Dmitri Anders has begun to make appearances at the house to see Vittoria and Emma. I'm still not sure how I feel about that, but I see how good it is for them to talk to someone who knew their mother. Who loved her so completely. I'm not a fan of his ties to the Russian mob but as long as he's in our territory, I'm not overly worried about it.

We've settled into our lives in Naples and we'll stay

here. Once the gossip about the massacre at the Ravello house dies down, we will sell the villa. I think it's for the best for everyone.

I stand at the patio window and watch Bastian and Vittoria walk onto the beach after their nightly swim. I smile to see them holding hands, laughing after Bastian stops to pick something out of her hair. I'm not sure I've ever seen my brother as happy as I see him now. Not even before, when we were children. He barely had a chance to be that anyway.

We reburied Geno Russo as Vittoria wanted. We did it for her, not for him. And I'm glad it's done, and she can move on. We all can. In the end, he's no less guilty of any crime in my eyes. His cowardice cost us all so much, Vittoria especially, and I won't forgive him those things.

I turn away from the window when Bastian and Vittoria enter the house and I hear her giggle as they approach the open study door.

"Isn't it getting cold for you to swim?" I ask Vittoria. My brother will keep this up year-round. You can't talk sense into him.

"A little," she says, wrapping herself around me and kissing me.

"Christ, you're freezing," I say, hugging her to me.

"It feels good to swim out in the sea at night," she says, looking up at me. "Clears my head."

"A cold shower will do the same." I wink and poke her nose. "Let's go get you into a hot bath." We have a routine. She swims with Bastian then I bathe her to warm her up. Win-win-win.

"Not yet," she says, her expression growing serious.

I exchange a glance with my brother as she takes my hand and Bastian's and sits up both down on the couch. She perches on my lap, sets her legs over Bastian's and leans her head into my chest.

"I'm happy, you know," she says. "I didn't realize I didn't know what to be happy meant all those years."

I kiss the top of her head tasting the salt of the sea. "I'm glad but we need to get you warmed up before you catch a cold."

"He's right," Bastian says, rubbing her feet.

"Are you happy?" she asks us, looking at us with what is almost worry in her eyes.

Again, Bastian and I exchange a glance. "What's going on, Dandelion?" Bastian asks.

"I'm asking if you're happy."

"Yes. I'm happy. You, brother?" he asks me.

I nod, rub her back. "What's on your mind, Vittoria?"

"You're both so great with Emma."

I raise my eyebrows.

"And she loves you both so much. I'm glad she has you in her life."

Bastian and I wait because she has something to say.

"She's young to be an aunt and I know it's soon. We haven't even talked about it, but…"

Shock stops my heart. It takes me a full minute to

process. I stare at her, and she can't seem to stop smiling.

"What are you saying?" Bastian finally asks, sounding off, not quite himself.

"I'm pregnant."

# EPILOGUE 3
## VITTORIA

*Five Months Later*

The Naples house is feeling more and more like home. Emma's toys and books are scattered throughout, and she is adjusting so well. She's enrolled in school, and her speaking is progressing by leaps and bounds. And she's easily picking up Italian. It helps that the brothers speak Italian with her while Nana and I stick to English.

The villa at Ravello has been sold, and I'm glad. I don't want Emma to see it again. To remember what happened there. And Nora still has nightmares of what she witnessed in that house.

It's a bright, clear morning, and I take a deep breath in. I love it here in Italy. I understand why my dad wanted so badly to come back.

The cemetery is deserted so early in the morning. Fog curls low around the gravestones, and I hug my wool jacket closer, putting a hand on my softly rounded belly. I walk toward my father's grave.

When I reach it, I crouch down in the soft, damp earth. I wipe mud from a recent storm off the carving of his name and pick the dandelions growing in the thick grass. I didn't bring flowers, so I lay those in a sort of bouquet. He would smile down on me to see it, but I doubt he's smiling today. He knows why I'm here.

I straighten and think about the man I knew, and tears warm my eyes. I hope he is at peace.

I don't know if Amadeo and Bastian realize how much it meant to me that they let me rebury my father. It symbolizes the closing of a chapter for me. I will mourn my father. I will miss him. And I accept that there are things I will never learn about him. But in a way, I don't want to know. Maybe that's cowardice on my part but it is the truth and it's the best I can do right now.

But there is one more thing.

I won't come back here after today. I can't. Burying my father properly will be my final act as his daughter. Now I am no longer that. I am Amadeo and Bastian's wife. Because I meant it about closing this chapter. His grave will be looked after. Fresh flowers delivered weekly. I arranged for it all. But anything else, after all that's happened, all that could have been prevented, I can't without feeling like I'm betraying those I love, those who are living.

"I love you, Daddy. I'll try to remember you as you were to me. And I will miss you," I tell him and let my tears drop into the earth. Do I forgive him? I don't know. From inside my coat pocket, I take out his ring. It's heavy in my hand. I set it on top of his grave, then lay my hand on the cool stone. "Goodbye."

Without a word, the brothers come to stand on either side of me. I don't look at them, not yet. This was my idea, not theirs. They wouldn't have asked this of me.

A cool wind blows and a wisp of hair slips from its pins. It's only here this happens. Nowhere else do the dropped leaves of this early fall day rustle. Just around us. Goose bumps rise on my arms, and I slip my hands into Amadeo's and Bastian's.

I don't know what my father wants to say as we turn and walk back toward our waiting SUV. Was it that he understands my decision? I'm going to think so. And as we climb into the back of the vehicle and Amadeo draws the seat belt over my shoulder, taking care to tuck it under my swelling belly, I feel her. For the first time, I feel our baby.

I must gasp because both Amadeo and Bastian stop.

"Dandelion?" Bastian asks. He hasn't stopped calling me that, but I don't mind.

I smile and nod as I set my hand over the spot where I feel it again. It's the lightest touch. A flutter of butterfly wings almost. It's gone as quickly as it came, and I turn to the brothers in turn.

"We'll name her Hannah," I say.

They exchange a glance. "Might be a boy," Amadeo says.

I shake my head. "She's a girl. And her name is going to be Hannah."

Amadeo tucks that strand of hair that blew away behind my ear and kisses my temple. "Hannah."

Bastian brushes his thumb under my eye and looks at me with those burning amber eyes.

"I like Hannah. But let's all agree. If it's a boy, it's Bastian."

We all laugh as the driver pulls out of the cemetery gates and we head home, together. Where I plan on living happily ever after with the men I love. The men I can't live without.

## BONUS EPILOGUE
VITTORIA

*The Birth of Hannah*

Emma and I are sitting on the patio, and she is reading to me from *The Gruffalo*. I'm not sure if she's actually reading or has memorized the text since we've read it so much for so many years, but I don't care. Her voice is music to my ears.

I rub my lower back as another contraction hits. They've been coming for days, but the doctor's assistant thought they were Braxton Hicks. Bastian insisted we go in and see the doctor rather than talk to the assistant, but I've put it off partly because I'm not sure I'm ready to let the baby go yet. Let her out of my control because right now, she's mine. No one can touch her. No one can hurt her.

I realize how that sounds. I know the brothers will never allow anything to happen to any of us, but I just want to keep her with me a little longer.

We won't find out if she's Amadeo's or Bastian's. It's a decision we made the night I told them I was pregnant.

Another contraction comes on the heels of the last one and I'm wondering if Bastian was right. If I should have seen the doctor. Neither he nor Amadeo loved the doctor's assistant, but they are overprotective, to say the least. I justified by telling them that my next appointment is in a few days and it's too early to deliver. Although technically, the baby is eight months along so it could happen.

Emma stops reading, sensing my discomfort even as I try not to show it. She puts the book aside and rubs my hard, round stomach.

"Is baby coming?" she asks.

"Not yet," I tell her as I straighten up and reach for my cup of tea on the table beside us. I almost have it to my mouth when another contraction worse than any I've had before hits. This time, I feel a warm gush of liquid between my legs, and my eyes go wide.

Emma's head tilts as she watches me.

"Vittoria?" she asks, worried.

I try to stand but double over with pain as water drips down my thighs.

"Get them," I tell her, trying not to scare her but failing as she bolts off her seat and runs inside.

I take a step to follow her, but the pain that comes with the next one is so sharp that I grab the table with both hands and squeeze my eyes shut.

"Vittoria!" It's Amadeo, followed closely by Bastian. They reach me at the same time and take hold of me before my knees give way from the pain.

"Call the doctor!" Bastian yells to Nora who appears at the door with Emma. I catch a glimpse of Emma's worried face. "Mom, call the doctor. Tell her Vittoria's water broke. We're going to the hospital."

The next thing I know I'm lifted into Amadeo's arms and carried through the house. I cry out as another contraction hits.

"How long have they been coming?" Bastian asks me.

"A while," I say. "They just... fuck... got bad a little bit ago."

"That fucking assistant," he grumbles as we head out the front door in record time, Bastian getting into the driver's seat as Amadeo sits in the back with me. I hold onto him as Bastian drives like a madman to the hospital.

"It's too soon," I say, feeling the moisture between my legs as I wait for the next painful wave.

"It'll be fine," Amadeo says but I see the worry on his face.

Everything is a blur as, once we arrive, I'm taken into a room and hooked up to machines. I can hear Bastian telling the doctor's assistant off just outside my door. The nurse pretends she doesn't hear a thing as Amadeo and Bastian enter the room, Amadeo with his arm around Bastian clearly to pull him away.

Bastian looks at me but all I can do is squeeze my eyes shut as the next contraction overwhelms me.

"Can't you give her something?" he snaps at the nurse.

"Doctor's on her way. She's just—"

Before she finishes, the door is pushed open, and Dr. Sandra enters. "I hear this little one is anxious to meet Mom!" she says with a wide smile for my benefit. She settles on a stool to check my progress.

"Give her something for the pain," Bastian tells her urgently.

Dr. Sandra looks up at him and shakes her head. "Too late. Baby's coming. Nurse."

Within minutes, the room is abuzz with men and women in scrubs. Before I know it, I'm being told to push, and fuck, the pain is so fucking bad all I see is black as I dig my nails into Amadeo and Bastian's hands and push until finally, what feels like a lifetime later, I hear her. I hear her little cry.

We all stop, and the doctor holds up a little pink human and smiles as the baby begins to wail, and I think she's the most beautiful thing I've ever seen.

"It's a girl," Dr. Sandra says.

And I look at her when they lay her on my chest and watch the awe on Amadeo and Bastian's faces as they take her in.

"Hannah," I whisper as Hannah wriggles and turns her face up to mine, and for the briefest of moments, her eyes meet mine before she closes them, and I know that I can't be happier than I am in this instant. This beautiful moment that marks the beginning of the rest of our lives.

# WHAT TO READ NEXT
DEVIL'S PAWN

*Isabelle*

A masquerade ball. What can be more beautiful? More perfect? Especially one put on by The Society.

Bouquets of flowers spill over tables set with the best china. Waiters serve champagne in crystal flutes and an eight-piece orchestra plays a waltz beneath the dazzling glow of a dozen chandeliers.

It's every girl's fantasy.

Every girl but me.

I stand in the shadows and watch the dancers. Men and women move together as if they've practiced this all their lives. I wonder if they are guests or professional dancers hired by The Society to add to the ambiance. I wouldn't be surprised if it was the latter because I'm pretty sure I didn't look like they do when

I danced with the stream of men my brother, Carlton, arranged for me.

I shudder at the thought of my last dance partner. A man old enough to be my grandfather.

A breeze blows into the grand Baroque ballroom as someone opens a window a few feet from me. The rain has slowed to a drizzle and the room is muggy even with the air conditioning running on high.

After a quick glance to confirm Carlton isn't watching, I drink the last of my champagne and set the empty flute on a nearby table. I slip quietly toward the exit and out the double French doors that stand open, in spite of the damp night.

In the courtyard, small tents have been erected to protect guests from the rain. They're decorated with warmly glowing lanterns and too many flowers to count. Men and women collect beneath the tents drinking, smoking their cigarettes and laughing too loudly.

Everyone turns to look at me as I pass. It's the dress. It's ridiculous with its feather skirt that barely reaches mid-thigh and the cinched waist of the corset top which is seriously limiting my oxygen supply. Carlton's choice. It showed all my best attributes apparently. At least the mask, which I liken to chainmail, leaves only my eyes on display.

The mask is pretty with it's delicate gold chains and coins brushing my shoulders with each step. And it offers some protection from curious eyes. The too-revealing dress I could do without.

Deciding to risk the drizzle that will likely make the feathers of my dress wilt, I hurry to the small chapel on the other side of the courtyard. No one will be there. I know that for sure. Society members may profess to be religious but from what I've seen, they're going through the motions. Showing up in their Sunday best, each outdoing the other, at least where fashion is concerned.

The wooden door is heavy. It creaks open just far enough to let me slip inside. I close it behind me and breathe a sigh of relief at the familiar sight, familiar scent. I miss incense when I'm away too long and Carlton isn't the church-going type.

I like this particular chapel especially. I have since I was little and my mom brought me with her when she cleaned the compound. I still remember sitting in the front pew, my legs too short for my feet to touch the floor. I remember how at home I felt when she sat me here to wait for her while she did her work.

I walk to that pew now, taking in the usual shadows of the place. The only light comes from candles lit along alcoves in the walls and those on the altar. When I get to the center of the aisle, I bow my head, make the sign of the cross, then take a seat. I slip off my shoes. The heels are too high and the fit too narrow. I touch the familiar carving in the pew. Two initials. *CY*.

It's the same seat I always take when I can get here. Right in the front row as if God could see me better for it. It's not that I ask for anything. I know better than that. It's not even that I pray. I just close my eyes and feel the silence here. The absolute absence of sound.

It's better than any masquerade ball. Better than dances with a hundred men as Carlton brokers a union that will benefit the family. I don't think it's crossed his mind what I want. Don't think he's considered the fact that while it may benefit his—*our*—family, it has already taken me off the course I'd set for myself years ago.

But I can't dwell. Not now. I need a reprieve and this chapel, these stolen moments, are it.

And so, I open my eyes and lift my gaze to the altar. One of the candles that is usually lit has blown out. I wonder if I did that when I walked in. I get up to relight it.

A creak along the back of the chapel startles me. I gasp, spin around. It's darkest there, just before the baptismal font. Almost pitch black. I peer into the shadows but see no movement, hear no other sound.

"Is someone there?" I ask, feeling silly when no one answers.

It's old wood creaking. That's all.

I turn back around, trying to ward off the chill that's clung to me all night. But I remind myself it's always cooler in the chapel and resume my walk to the altar. There, I find the book of matches and strike one. The flame glows bright and I have to stand on tiptoe to reach the wick of the tall candle.

Soon it's lit and I'm blowing out the match when

the sound of laughter from just beyond the door disrupts the peace of this place. Before I know it, the chapel door slams against the wall.

I jump.

Two men stumble in, laughing as they do, and one rushes to shove the door closed behind him. With them they bring the stench of alcohol and weed. The moment I see their faces, I'm sure they're both high. I can see it in their red eyes, in the flush of their skin, hear it in their strange, giddy laughter.

I'd guess them to be twenty, twenty-one maybe. Just a year or two older than me. And I recognize one of them. I danced with him not one hour ago. Although I can't recall his name. Only that I didn't like him. Didn't like the way his fingers caressed the exposed skin of my back as he spun me around the dance floor.

"There she is," he says, as if recognizing me, too. His mask is pushed to the top of his head and he licks his lips, allowing his gaze to linger at the swell of my breasts above the bodice of the dress. "That's the girl," he tells his companion with a nudge of his elbow.

The other ones eyes are locked on me, mouth hard, set in an ugly line.

"The Bishop girl," he says. Both come closer, one stopping behind me. "Half-Bishop," he clarifies.

"The right half," the other one says, and they both laugh although I don't get the joke. "Let's get that thing off your head so we can get a proper look at you," he says, reaching for the clip holding my mask in place.

"I don't think so," I tell him, stepping out of his reach but in doing so cornering myself against the altar.

"Why not? I wouldn't make a deal with your brother sight unseen. You never know, am I right?"

"I think Manson is the one making the deal, bro," his friend says and makes a face.

He reaches again and this time when he gets his fingers in my hair I shove at him with both hands, managing to push him backward. He's off balance because he's both high and drunk. I realize how much more dangerous that makes him when his eyes narrow to angry slits as his friend laughs.

"Excuse me, I need to get back," I say, turning to slip away, managing to take a step before he catches my arm.

I stop, look at his hand then up at him. I paste a smile on my face and step closer. My heart thuds against my chest. I'm not sure if I'm more angry or afraid but I know two things.

First, I need to get away from these two or it's not going to bode well for me. And second, I cannot show my fear no matter what. Some men get a high from that alone.

"My brother is on his way. He won't like you putting your hands on me," I say.

"I wouldn't call this putting my hands on you," he says, then turns to his friend. "Would you?"

His friend shakes his head. "Nope."

"Now this I'd call putting my hands on you," the one who has hold of me says, turning me slightly and slapping my ass so hard that I stumble forward. It makes both men erupt in laughter as his grip around my arm tightens.

But that's when I hear that same sound I heard before. Coming from the same shadowy corner. Except this time, it's not creaking wood.

Something moves when I look to the spot.

Dust motes dance in candlelight, but the two who barged into the chapel don't notice the shift in the air until we hear the footfalls. They turn and we all watch as the darkness takes form and begins to move toward us.

My heart pounds against my chest and for a moment, I'm not sure if it's man or beast for the shadow it casts. But then I recognize the long black cloak of the Sovereign Sons. It billows around the man making that darkness following him even bigger, more frightening.

He's too tall. Too broad-shouldered. Everything about him too dark, from the black-on-black beneath the traditional cloak, to the horned mask hiding his face, to the fury directed at the men who've cornered me.

He doesn't bother with words. He simply steps toward us, the two looking like boys as he looms closer, towering over them in build and height and sheer presence. He glances only momentarily at me before his eyes hone in on the one grasping my arm. It seems to take no effort at all for him to pry the man's hand off me. My tormentor's face contorts in pain as the masked stranger twists his arm behind his back. His friend backs away one step, two before running for the door.

"What the fuck, man?" cries the one who can't run. "Let go!"

The stranger twists a little more.

"She's not yours to break," he whispers, voice low and hard.

I process the words, shudder at the strange sense of foreshadowing.

I realize I've backed up against the altar. I'm staring, mouth gaping, heart racing. And I see what the mask he's wearing portrays. Some sort of horned beast. A devil.

But it's when he pins me with his gaze that something drops to my stomach, possibly my heart, because I stop thinking. Stop breathing.

I stare back into the darkest eyes I've ever seen.

*Danger.*

It's the only thought I have. The single word my mind can muster.

One of his eyes is midnight blue, the other a steely gray. And his gaze is full of something so malevolent, I feel it like fire burning my flesh.

It's an eternity before he releases me from his gaze and simultaneously shoves the drunk man toward the door. A moment later I'm alone with the masked stranger.

He'd been here all along. Sitting in the shadows silently watching me.

All night I'd felt it. Eyes on me. All night I'd felt that chill. I shudder now because it was him. This masked man. I recognize the sensation, the unease. That sense of being exposed. Alone in a room full of people.

My mouth goes dry. I press my back to the altar, hands clutching the edge of it.

His gaze roams over me leaving goose bumps in its wake. I shudder. He must see it. Must realize I'm terrified. And only when he takes a step back are my lungs able to work again. Am I able to draw breath again.

"You shouldn't be in here alone," he says. "It's not safe for a woman alone when there's alcohol and idiots about."

I stare up at him, stupefied.

"Your shoes," he says.

"What?" I ask, my voice a whisper.

He gestures down and I look at my bare feet, then up at him. I point to where I'd left them. He gets my shoes and carries them back to me. He stands just a little too close, too much in my space like it's his, like it belongs to him and I'm the invader.

I still can't seem to move.

"I won't eat you," he says in that low, rumbling voice.

My chest shudders with a deep breath. I tell myself to relax. It's nothing. He just saved me. What I felt, that chill, it's just my imagination.

"Not yet anyway," he says, and I know he's grinning beneath his mask.

I swallow. I'm shaking.

He bends to set my shoes on the floor. I take in the sheer size of him. He's easily twice as big as me. He straightens and holds out his hand, palm up. Along his wrist I see the creeping of a tattoo. A serpent's tail.

I'm staring. It takes all I have to drag my gaze up to his.

"Put your shoes on," he says.

My throat is too dry to speak, to form words or make sound, so I slip my hand into his and gasp at the sudden shock.

He closes his fingers around mine and I feel the sheer power in the palm of his hand as he holds me steady. He studies me for a long, long moment before I blink, lowering my gaze and slipping on my shoes.

"Good," he says, and I just keep standing there, my hand trapped inside his.

The gong announcing dinner rings. I look up at him.

He lets his gaze drop to my lips, then lower, to the swell of my breasts. Sweat slides down the back of my neck. He releases my hand and cups the gold chains hanging from my mask as if weighing them, his eyebrows furrowing.

"Isabelle Bishop," he says, looking at me again.

He knows my name. How does he know my name?

The gong sounds a second time. And, after long moments of silence, a third.

He steps backward.

"Go back to the party, Isabelle Bishop, and remember to keep out of dark rooms. You never know who's lying in wait."

Devil's Pawn is Available in all stores now!

# ALSO BY NATASHA KNIGHT

*Ruined Kingdom Duet*

Ruined Kingdom

Broken Queen

*The Devil's Pawn Duet*

Devil's Pawn

Devil's Redemption

*To Have and To Hold*

With This Ring

I Thee Take

Stolen: Dante's Vow

*The Society Trilogy*

Requiem of the Soul

Reparation of Sin

Resurrection of the Heart

*The Rite Trilogy*

His Rule

Her Rebellion

Their Reign

*Dark Legacy Trilogy*

Taken (Dark Legacy, Book 1)

Torn (Dark Legacy, Book 2)

Twisted (Dark Legacy, Book 3)

*Unholy Union Duet*

Unholy Union

Unholy Intent

*Collateral Damage Duet*

Collateral: an Arranged Marriage Mafia Romance

Damage: an Arranged Marriage Mafia Romance

*Ties that Bind Duet*

Mine

His

*MacLeod Brothers*

Devil's Bargain

*Benedetti Mafia World*

Salvatore: a Dark Mafia Romance

Dominic: a Dark Mafia Romance

Sergio: a Dark Mafia Romance

The Benedetti Brothers Box Set (Contains Salvatore, Dominic and Sergio)

Killian: a Dark Mafia Romance

Giovanni: a Dark Mafia Romance

*The Amado Brothers*

Dishonorable

Disgraced

Unhinged

*Standalone Dark Romance*

Descent

Deviant

Beautiful Liar

Retribution

Theirs To Take

Captive, Mine

Alpha

Given to the Savage

Taken by the Beast

Claimed by the Beast

Captive's Desire

Protective Custody

Amy's Strict Doctor

Taming Emma

Taming Megan

Taming Naia

Reclaiming Sophie

The Firefighter's Girl

Dangerous Defiance

Her Rogue Knight

Taught To Kneel

Tamed: the Roark Brothers Trilogy

## ABOUT THE AUTHOR

Natasha Knight is the *USA Today* Bestselling author of Romantic Suspense and Dark Romance Novels. She has sold over a million books and is translated into six languages. She currently lives in The Netherlands with her husband and two daughters and when she's not writing, she's walking in the woods listening to a book, sitting in a corner reading or off exploring the world as often as she can get away.

Contact Natasha here: natasha@natasha-knight.com

NATASHA KNIGHT

www.natasha-knight.com

Printed in Great Britain
by Amazon